Reluctant Tin Star

When Marshal Troy Garrison is forced to leave the Colorado town of Aguilar under a cloud, he figured he was done with the law for good. Shamed and humiliated through no fault of his own he heads south into New Mexico. A meeting with an itinerant gambler finds the unlikely travelling companions in Cimarron.

A series of unsavoury incidents culminating in Troy's rescue of a damsel in distress finds him reluctantly pinning on the tin star once again. An unscrupulous gang of rustlers is terrorizing the area. And Troy is forced to choose between the girl of his dreams and upholding the law when her brother becomes involved with the gang. Unfortunately, a man's past has a habit of catching him unawares. The havoc this causes will need all of the reluctant tin star's daring and ingenuity to overcome.

Reluctant Tin Star

Dale Graham

A Black Horse Western

ROBERT HALE

© Dale Graham 2017
First published in Great Britain 2017

ISBN 978-0-7198-2200-1

The Crowood Press
The Stable Block
Crowood Lane
Ramsbury
Marlborough
Wiltshire SN8 2HR

www.bhwesterns.com

Robert Hale is an imprint
of The Crowood Press

The right of Dale Graham to be identified as
author of this work has been asserted by him
in accordance with the Copyright, Designs and
Patents Act 1988

Typeset by
Derek Doyle & Associates, Shaw Heath
Printed and bound in Great Britain by
CPI Group (UK) Ltd, Croydon, CR0 4YY

ONE

ROLLING STONES

The lone rider emerged from the enclosing confines of Bluebottle Canyon and pushed his sturdy bay mare to the gallop. The horse was eager to stretch her legs for a spell. And Troy Garrison needed to clear the mush from his head. Too much whiskey the night before had addled his brain. There were things scrambling around inside that needed exorcising. And at that moment whiskey had seemed like the only cure. He had regretted that decision on waking up the next morning.

Not normally a man who resorted to hard liquor to assuage a troubled mind, Troy reckoned he had good reason. But such a dicey means of solving problems rarely amounted to anything other than misgivings. These were now being painfully resurrected as the demons once again reasserted their presence. 'Never again,' he muttered under his breath before uttering a morbid chuckle. How many times had a man made that promise?

Troy's disturbing exit from the Colorado town of Aguilar would have turned any man to the demon drink. At least the soporific effects of hard liquor had enabled him to forget, if only for the few hours of darkness. Three cups of strong coffee at daybreak had helped somewhat. Although they couldn't allay the iron hammer pounding relentlessly inside his skull. Only a good ride would do that. Man and beast thundered across the rolling grasslands. The wind in Troy's face, the clear morning air, both felt heady and invigorating.

Only the love of a good woman offered a better panacea when a man was feeling low. On more than one occasion he had figured to have found one for life. All had deserted him when he refused to abandon his profession. Such was the tenuous line between life and death that a dedicated lawman had to walk.

A growl of anger emerged from between clenched teeth, a biting wail plucked away on the early morning breeze. And it was all down to that bastard Isaac Dooley. Hence it was that the further from Aguilar he rode, the better he felt. What he couldn't escape was the humiliation those skunks had heaped upon the tough lawman. For Troy Garrison, town marshal of Aguilar, had been forced to quit under the most irksome of circumstances. Sure he could have stayed and toughed it out. But Troy refused to toady to anybody's behest, least of all that snake of a mayor who had bought the town council to further his own ends.

Again his teeth ground in a fresh spate of indignation. Over the next few hours, he tried to concentrate on the notion of a fresh start, a new beginning far away from Aguilar. Around noon he crossed the border into New Mexico. A faded signboard pinned to a tree was all that indicated he had now left Colorado. And good riddance.

That was when he noticed the plume of smoke snaking up out of a dip in the ground some distance ahead. Must be a camp of some sort. And he could sure use a cup of coffee, not to mention some vittles if'n they were available. Forced to leave Aguilar in a hurry, there had been no time for anything other than flight. Luckily a detailed knowledge of the terrain had enabled the fugitive to evade his pursuers.

He slowed the bay to a trot, then a walk as he neared the hidden pitch. A few yards back from the downfall, he stopped, a hand straying to the gun on his hip. It always paid to be wary when approaching an unknown bivouac.

'Coffee's on the boil, if'n you've a mind,' a cheery voice called out before Troy could announce his presence. The ex-lawman frowned, nudging the bay down into the hollow where a lone camper was standing with a blackened pot in one hand and a tin cup in the other. 'There's some rabbit stew on the boil as well. You're welcome to share the feast, such as it is.'

'Much obliged,' the newcomer replied. Caution

7

laced his chary reaction while stepping down and ground-hitching his cayuse. A hawkish gaze never left the nattily clad traveller. 'You must have mighty good hearing. I barely made a sound approaching your camp.'

'Known someone was a-coming since you crested that last ridge back yonder,' the man explained while pouring out the coffee which he handed across. 'Look, listen and never drink too much hard liquor. That's my motto.' Troy could certainly empathize with the latter piece of wisdom. 'Always pays for a guy in my profession to have all his senses tuned up.'

'And what might that be?' the newcomer posed, gratefully sipping the hot liquid. Although he had already guessed from the garish if somewhat shabby duds the guy was wearing.

The man tapped his tilted derby. 'See this? The King of Clubs, my lucky card. Fairplay's the name, gambling's my game – anything you fancy, poker, blackjack, penny-ante, even craps.' He flipped a pair of dice into the air catching them one-handed. 'You name it, I play it.'

Troy nodded, his supposition having been proved correct. A barely disguised wry smile broke across the stoic demeanour as he sat down. 'Mighty interesting. But does the name fit the player?' His thoughts briefly flashed back to a previous life, now hopefully put behind him.

'Honest Hal, that's me,' the jaunty card wielder intoned smugly while smoothing out the creases of his nifty silk vest. 'Although there are those who

8

sometimes can't get it into their thick skulls that the best players don't need to cheat. It's my proud boast, mister, that if'n I can't beat a fella squarely, it's me that's at fault. I clearly haven't read the signs right. When that happens it's best to throw in the towel and start up again elsewhere.' He eyed the newcomer over his coffee cup. 'Didn't quite catch your name, stranger?'

'Maybe that's cos I never gave it.' Troy remained silent.

The camper's right eyebrow lifted. This guy was not exactly what you would call the outgoing type. 'In that case, perhaps I should just call you *Mister*. So where you from Mr *Mister*? If'n that isn't too impertinent a question.'

Troy was not a man prone to revealing his past, nor his present. And the future would have to take care of itself. But nevertheless he gave the witty riposte an expressive nod. Fairplay's grin-cloaked features received a considered appraisal. He pondered awhile. Maybe he was being a mite too suspicious of his fellow traveller. After all, the gambler appeared to be just that, a likeminded rolling stone heading in the same direction.

Yet still he maintained a terse silence. After all he had good reason not to trust his fellow man. But Fairplay was not about to give up. A further attempt was made to fill the tense void. 'I was hoping for some companionable conversation. A drink, a bite to eat, maybe a game of cards. A guy gets kinda lonesome just talking to himself and his horse all the time. I could have kept quiet and allowed you to pass by on the far side of the ridge. Don't that mean something?'

Troy relented, as much as he considered was necessary. The guy had a point. 'The name is Troy Garrison. And I ain't normally a gambling man.' A gimlet eye held the other man in its poignant grip. 'As you have so eloquently explained, *Mr* Fairplay, the only winner in your line of work is the one who wears a King of Clubs in his hat.'

'Guess I asked for that,' was the contrite reply. Yet like a galling itch, he still persisted. 'Won't you even go for a simple game of rummy? We can play for match sticks if'n you like.'

Troy laughed. 'You just don't give up, do you?'

Fairplay shrugged. 'Gambling's in my blood. Don't know anything else. I was taught rummy by my pa at the age of six. Picked it up like a dog attracts fleas.' Once again the lilting southern drawl brought a half smile to Troy's craggy features. 'After the first half hour I had taken the old devil for twenty dollars. By the age of twelve there was nobody in town willing to sit in a game when young Harold was dealing. I've been playing the tables ever since.'

The listener could well believe the gambler's claim. A lazy right eye gave his features a lob-sided appearance likely to fox any opponent hoping to gain an advantage. It provided the classic poker face.

The observation took him back to another gambler he had known where a harelip had afforded a similar benefit. Unfortunately for Montana Red, his luck had run out when he made the mistake of playing poker with Sheb Dooley. Troy's eyes misted over at the recollection of why he happened to be sitting here right now, drinking coffee with a gambler in the middle of nowhere.

He shook off the traumatic remembrance. 'Guess you must be on the trail now due to a bad spell.'

'Your supposition is correct, sir,' Fairplay concurred with a regretful shake of the head. He gave the remark a rueful sigh. 'Met my match in a fellow sportsman in Branson. Read him all wrong, a most unusual lapse of concentration, and he cleared me out. But it sure taught me a thing or two.' He paused, drawing on his cigar as Troy waited for the finale. 'I won't never take anybody for granted again. Now all I got are the clothes I'm wearing, a horse and saddle, with just about enough grub to get me to the next town.'

Now it was Fairplay's turn to critically inspect his reluctant companion. 'Garrison you say? Seems like I've heard that name before. As I recall, a lawman with that handle was involved in a fracas up north apiece. Wouldn't by any chance be related to you, would he?'

Troy's face darkened. News sure travelled fast. The new telegraph had a lot to answer for. He drew hard on the cigar that Fairplay had given him. Thin lips tightened in frustration, teeth grinding like an angry dog. The dancing flames of the camp fire reflected the anguish gripping his innards before he felt able to respond. The words that emerged assumed a guttural rasp. 'No relation, mister. We're one and the same.'

11

Fairplay shrunk back recognizing that his inquisitive nature had ventured into turbulent waters. 'Seems like I struck a bum note, Mr Garrison. Maybe I should keep my big mouth shut.' The gambler's apology was genuinely repentant. 'Sorry for intruding. A guy has a right to keep his own business private. I ought never to have stepped out of line.'

Troy waved the extenuation away. Maybe getting the obnoxious episode off his chest would be good for the soul. Help him to move on. It was barely ten days since he had been forced to quit Aguilar under a cloud that was not of his making. That was the hard part. Doing his job, the job of keeping law and order that he had so much valued had been made impossible.

He stared into the flickering embers of the dancing flames. A shiver of resentment rippled through the muscles of his taut frame.

TWO

TROUBLE BREWING

Marshal Troy Garrison was busy filling in a form detailing all the incidents he had attended during the previous month. It was an irksome chore but one demanded by the Sheriff's Office based at the Las Animas county seat of Trinidad. His attention was abruptly interrupted by the bartender from the Pioneer saloon who barged through the door uninvited.

The unexpected arrival drew a caustic frown across the lawman's face. 'Don't you ever think to knock afore busting into a guy's office?' he snapped out.

The rebuke was ignored. 'Montana Red's been shot down over a game of poker,' the panting barfly blurted out as he paused to draw breath. He had run

13

down the street at a fair lick to deliver the chilling news. No mean feat for a portly jasper of Smiler Dan Springer's hefty bulk. But there was no cheery beam creasing his rubicund features now. 'I've sent for Doc Sweeney. But I ain't holding out much hope for Red's chances.'

At that moment, the forlorn account was interrupted. On hearing the name, Harold Fairplay sat up. He was now all ears. 'I know Red Staple,' he declared. 'I sat in on one of his games up in Denver. The guy's straight as a dye. As I recall we both came out even. The killer must have been a sore loser with too much liquor inside him. Red should never have allowed the soused-up critter to join the game.' He shook his head in reprimanding commiseration. 'Inviting guys like that to join a game is asking for trouble.'

Troy scowled at Fairplay's candid but truthful response. But he did not look up as he carried on with the grim revelation.

For a brief instant the marshal was taken aback by the unsettling revelation conveyed by Smiler Dan. This was not just any old shooting fracas. In keeping with his current companion, Troy Garrison also had very good reason to believe that the gambler in question operated a clean game.

If a lawman had any friends it was highly unlikely they would have included a gambler. Yet he and Montana Red Staple had taken to each other like bees to honey. The guy's ready wit and obvious lack of any sly intrigue fascinated the lawman. It was a

14

rare combination in a card wielder. Staple was greatly respected by those who frequented gambling halls. Indeed those who lost invariably held no grudge against the jovial dealer.

Troy occasionally sat in on games and never had any doubts as to his friend's veracity. He had often marvelled at the manner in which the guy managed to smooth over other gamblers' losses. It was natural that some fellas would grumble about losing their poke. That was human nature. But thus far that was all they had amounted to. And the gambler always tried to warn off guys who were getting in over their heads.

Now and again it had occurred to the marshal that in following such a profession a time would invariably come when Red Staple's luck ran out. And it had finally happened on Troy Garrison's turf.

'Who shot him down?' was the obvious initial enquiry he asked of Springer as he buckled on the tooled leather gun belt and checked the load of his .44 Colt Frontier. The barman ignored the question, burbling on about how Staple had attracted a more refined breed of gambler to the Pioneer. Now trade would revert back to the riff-raff of before.

Again the question was posed, this time in a much more stentorian bark making the barman jump six inches into the air. 'Out with it, Dan, who killed him?'

The usual beaming grin had been well and truly wiped off the ruddy face as he gulped nervously. 'It was Sheb Dooley. And he's over at the Pioneer right

15

now claiming that Red was dealing from the bottom of the deck and he had every right to gun the cheating bastard down.' The barman held up a placatory hand seeing the icy glint in Garrison's regard. 'Those were his words, Marshal, not mine.'

Sheb Dooley. He might have known it would be that skunk. The guy figured himself to be a big shot in Aguilar. Troy had tangled with him on numerous occasions before. Misdemeanours that had been punished with fines paid by his father who just happened to be the town mayor and chairman of the council.

But this was something else. A killing was only answerable through a court of law presided over by a territorial judge. No way could Isaac Dooley buy off his wayward son's freedom this time.

'You get back to the Pioneer and keep an eye on the critter,' Troy directed the barman. 'While you're passing, call in at Joe Finch's saddle shop and have him send young Jimmy round. I need him to look after the jailhouse while I'm out of the office. There are two jaspers cooling their heels in the cellblock. And I don't want them getting any bright ideas about trying to bust out while I'm away.'

Jimmy Finch had pestered Troy to take him on as a deputy in training much to the chagrin of his ma. But the boy was adamant that he wanted to be a lawman. His father had agreed to a trial period on a part-time basis until such time as Jimmy was old enough to take up the job full time after his eighteenth birthday.

The kid was big for his age, and had proved to be a keen apprentice. He was no slouch when it came to the rough stuff either. A mean right hook had taken down tough cowpokes twice his size.

Handling a revolver had proved second nature to the boy. Although Troy was always around to ensure the youngster did not come to any harm. Right from the start, he had laid it on thick that any real gunplay should be left to him alone. The last thing Troy Garrison needed was having to answer to Martha Finch for his failure to keep her only son safe from harm.

Keeping watch over a couple of rowdy drunks like the Basford twins should prove no problem for the boy. So when Jimmy arrived some five minutes later, Troy emphasized that on no account should he get into conversation with the wily duo. 'Those guys will figure they can bribe their way out of jail by offering you a fistful of dollars. Any dough they possess will be paying their fines.'

'Don't you worry none, Marshal,' Jimmy declared in a serious vein while hitching up his gun belt. 'No pair of two-bit hotheads will get the better of Deputy Finch.' He uttered the last two words with pride squaring his youthful yet beefy shoulders to prove he could be trusted. 'They ain't going no place.'

Troy gave a perceptive nod struggling to hide the smile that threatened to deflate the youngster's enthusiasm. 'I know I can count on you, Jimmy, while I investigate this shooting at the Pioneer.' The kid preened like a strutting rooster at the praise from this highly respected figure.

17

And with the matter sorted to his satisfaction, Troy Garrison departed. Yet not without some trepidation. If truth be told, the marshal had been anticipating such an occurrence for some time. Over the last few months, the brash tearaway had been goading him. Backed up by his buddies, Dooley tossed insults his way like confetti in the wind. His aim was to make the unflappable lawman lose his temper.

When that failed he upped the ante, spreading the word that Troy was nought but a milksop. As the mayor's irresponsible only son, Sheb Dooley reckoned he was untouchable. Well, now he was going to find that no man was above the law, least of all a worthless no-good like him.

Troy had resisted the urge to beat the braggart to a pulp. Such a reaction would have brought fleeting satisfaction only; more than likely a heap of trouble from the authorities who paid his wages. Everybody was answerable to the written law, especially those who purported to uphold it. And so he had held his temper in check.

Until now. Troy was seething. This time, Dooley had gone too far. He stamped along the boardwalk, crossing the street, eyes set firmly on the batwing doors of the Pioneer saloon. Folks stepped aside. Nobody wanted to feel the wrath of the tough lawdog when he was in a fighting mood.

He paused at the entrance to the saloon to draw breath and calm his simmering anger. Then he pushed inside. The noise of two dozen voices suddenly quieted as all eyes swung towards the

newcomer. Dooley was standing at the bar surrounded by his laughing pals. But the glowering look
pasted onto the lawman's face caused them to pull
away from the source of his ire.

'Well, if'n it ain't the big man himself,' Dooley
slurred, levering himself off the bar. 'You're a bit late
to arrest that tinhorn over yonder.' A flapping arm
waved towards the dead body of Montana Red which
was lying face down across a green baize table. 'I've
already done the job for you.' He spat on the straw
covered floor. 'No sneaky cardsharp gets the better
of Sheb Dooley.'

Troy walked across to where the killer was standing. Dooley suddenly found himself isolated. Nobody
wanted to be in the firing line when the lead started
flying. Troy held out his hand. 'I'll take that gun,
kid,' he hissed out. 'You're under arrest for the
murder of an innocent man.'

Dooley guffawed. 'Innocent? Who you trying to
fool? That skunk swindled me out of a hefty poke. He
was dealing from the bottom. And I caught him out.
Ain't that true, boys?' But the slurred appeal to his
cronies fell on deaf ears.

The marshal took a step closer. 'Red Staple was
honest as the day is long. I'd trust him with my life.
And you're gonna pay big time for his killing. Now
hand over that gun!'

Dooley growled, hunching down ready for the
challenge. Had he been sober, such a rash intention
would have doubtless ended in a sneering climb-
down. But the drink had made him reckless beyond

any such responsible judgment. His hand dropped to the holstered revolver, fingers groping ineptly to draw the gun.

Troy coughed out a mocking snigger at the ham-fisted braggart's clumsiness. In the flick of a gnat's wing, his own gun leapt into his hand connecting with the killer's head. Dooley slumped to the ground, out cold. The marshal stepped back, the panned revolver covering Dooley's buddies should they be considering any support for their fallen comrade. But the marshal's blunt and highly effective response to Dooley's challenge was enough to stifle any retaliation.

Troy snapped out orders to the nearest of Dooley's associates. 'You two carry this lump of dog dirt over to the jailhouse, pronto.'

The blunt stipulation saw the nervous minions following the marshal out of the saloon toting the body of their apprehended buddy. As soon as the grim deputation had left the saloon, a noisy babble broke out as men eagerly discussed the outcome of the brutal episode. Bets were exchanged as to how long Dooley would be in jail. Everybody was well aware that the mayor would not take the arrest of his hotshot son lying down. Sparks were bound to fly in the town of Aguilar in the days ahead.

Within minutes of his kin being roughly tossed into his new accommodation, Isaac Dooley was being fully apprised of the situation. The mayor angrily stamped around his office above the council premises. 'Why didn't you yellow bellies have the guts

to help him out?' the official railed, his flushed countenance redder than usual. 'I pay you enough to
keep Sheb out of trouble and this is what happens.'
His livid gaze pinned down a thin beanpole called
Stringer.

'We had no idea he was going to blow up like that,'
the lanky dogsbody griped appealing to his other two
associates, who were nervously shuffling their feet.
'Ain't that the truth of it, boys?'

'Stringer's right, boss. Sheb took us all by surprise,' a short stocky dude called Chuck Ryker avidly
concurred, uneasily fingering his hat. 'One minute
he was hunched over his cards, the next all hell
breaks loose. Next thing we know, Staple is lying
there, dead as a doorpost.'

The third man, a shifty-eyed jasper known as
Three-Fingered Dick Blezzard, felt it prudent to add
his support to the plethora of excuses. 'Montana Red
must have been cheating for Sheb to go off half-
cocked like that. There can't be any other
explanation.' He looked to the others for their con-
sensus. A series of hurried nods backed up the
assertion.

But Mayor Dooley had other ideas. He knew full
well that his son was more than likely to blame
someone else for his own bungling ineptitude where
card-playing skill was involved. But he kept that
notion to himself. 'You're right there, boys. Sheb
would never have cheated.'

More eager nods greeted this support of their
dubious claim. 'So what we gonna do about it, boss?'

Stringer asked, relieved that any blame had been shifted off the shoulders of him and his buddies.

It didn't seem to make any difference to the mayor that his no-account son had shot a man for allegedly cheating at cards. In Dooley's eyes, gamblers were the lowest form of life and didn't merit the same rights as respectable citizens. A dead tinhorn was no loss to the world.

But he was astute enough to recognize that such a view could not be bandied around by an elected official dependent on the good will of the local populace. He could not be seen to favour his own kin without just cause. This delicate situation would need to be handled carefully. Otherwise, Sheb would be facing a trial chaired by the infamous Hanging Judge Ephraim Parker.

And Blezzard had put his finger on the button. If'n he could persuade folks that Red Staple was the guilty party, then this issue need never come to trial.

The mayor was, however, well aware that this particular gambler was a friend of that stuffed shirt of a marshal. Montana Red Staple had garnered a solid reputation for running an honest game. Various reputable members of the council would vouch for his veracity if called to the witness stand. Sheb would not have a leg to stand on if brought to trial. The mayor's close-set beady eyes glittered like sparkling ice crystals. Something had to be done to ensure that never happened.

The circuit judge was not expected in Animas County until the end of the month. Sessions were held in the county seat at Trinidad. Isaac had two weeks to overturn his son's arrest. He dismissed the hovering lackeys with a casual wave of the hand. 'This needs thinking on, boys. I'll let you know what's to be done later.'

A dark frown creased the broad forehead. Isaac slumped into a chair. He grabbed a bottle of whiskey from a drawer in his desk and sunk a hefty belt. 'You crazy young fool,' he muttered to himself. 'Why did you have to gun down an honest gambler like Red Staple? This is gonna cost me a heap of dough to put right.'

Already the mayor's devious mind was working on a plan to seal his son's release from custody. But he would need to be careful. First job was to speak with Sheb and get his side of the incident. Setting his hat straight, the official vacated his office and hustled across the street to the jailhouse. Without knocking, he barged straight in.

'Don't nobody have any manners these days?' grumbled the incumbent lawman who had been lambasting his prisoner. His two previous guests had been released on bail with the proviso that they fork out a ten-dollar fine each by the end of the week or spend a month in jail. He had no wish to have three miscreants in the cell block together. That would be inviting more trouble than he needed at the moment.

Dooley immediately apologized, having no wish to antagonize the steadfast starpacker. 'Sorry about that, Marshal. But I'm worried about Sheb. Him being accused of murder has hit me hard. I know he can be a bit of a hothead, but being locked up for killing a guy when he had due cause don't seem fair.'

Troy stiffened. 'Red Staple getting a belly full of hot lead while pursuing his lawful profession, now that ain't what I call fair. And it was your boy that pulled the trigger. No question about that.'

'How do you know that Staple was playing a straight game? Sheb don't cheat. So I reckon it was the tinhorn who was double-dealing.' Dooley's prominent chin jutted forward as he attempted to lay stress on his claim. 'And I can gather witnesses who will testify that the varmint was not so clean as he'd like us all to believe.'

'Guys like Stringer and Three-Fingered Dick, I suppose,' sneered the cynical lawman who was becoming a mite tired of the mayor's hectoring tone. 'If'n you think Judge Parker will believe the testimonies of rats like that, you're pissing into the wind.' He slung a thumb towards the cell block. 'The skunk stays in there until I can escort him to Trinidad. Then we'll see who's telling the truth.'

Dooley huffed and puffed some. 'Don't forget it was me who advised the council to hire you in the first place. I reckon you should give some loyalty to those who pay your wages.' Garrison's stern features remained unmoved by the appeal. So Dooley tried changing tactics. 'It's clear to me, Marshal, that you've never had kids. A female grizzly bear will fight tooth and nail to protect her cubs. And it's the same with humans. What if'n I was to offer you an extra

24

twenty bucks a month. Would that make you more co-operative?'

That was the last straw for the scrupulous lawman. He grabbed a-hold of the irksome official and shook him like a dog with a bone. 'Figure everybody is like you. Is that it, Dooley? Well bribery is not going to get you anywhere while I'm administering the law in Aguilar. Now get out of this office before I kick you out.'

Shaken by the assault on his person, Dooley broke free and backed off. He wagged a finger under Troy's nose. 'This time you've gone too far, Garrison. I'll have your job for this. Then we'll see who runs things around here. As mayor I have the authority to decide what the law is. And I intend to do just that.'

'Is that a threat, Mr Mayor?' the stubborn-willed lawdog growled.

'Take it any way you want. One thing's for sure. My boy ain't gonna dance to any hangman's tune.'

Troy bundled the irate official out of the office. 'That's exactly what will happen if'n the law takes its proper course. Until then, you'd be well advised to keep out of my way,' he rapped out, slamming the door.

'I heard all that, Marshal,' a guffawing voice warbled from inside the cell block. Sheb Dooley was in raptures at his father's threatening manner. 'My pa sure is in a right lather. Never figured the old stroke had it in him. You've discovered that he don't take kindly to having his authority challenged. I reckon a week at the most and he'll have me out of this dump. Just like you. It'll be interesting to see how that kid Jimmy Finch handles being a starpacker. Mighty interesting, I'd say.'

Troy gritted his teeth. 'That lump on your head not enough, Dooley?' he snarled, struggling against an overwhelming desire to go back there and lay his hogleg across the crowing braggart's skull once again. Yet somehow he managed to contain the irresistible urge. Resorting to physical violence under these circumstances would only play into the hands of that pompous low life of a mayor.

The marshal knew he was in the right here. A murder had been committed and the law would take its course. Of that he was determined. Although he would need to amass a plethora of prosecution witnesses who were prepared to testify as to Montana Red's honesty and Sheb Dooley's dissolute reputation. Troy had no doubt that Dooley senior would attempt to pull some underhanded stunt to free his son from the just deserts he had coming. The lawman would need to be on his guard until such time as the whole matter could be passed on to a higher authority.

A couple of days passed with no hint of the trouble Isaac Dooley had threatened. Perhaps the mayor had resigned himself to the inevitable. One could only live in hope, the marshal mused. His deputy chose that moment to enter the office having been to investigate some hens that were rampaging over a neighbour's vegetable patch. Since the shooting of Montana Red, the impending murder trial was hanging over the small town like a black thunder cloud. The talk was of nothing else.

'You look a mite troubled, Marshal,' the youngster remarked noting his superior's disconsolate slump of the normally squared shoulders. 'Can't say that I blame you. The atmosphere out there is mighty tense. It feels like folks are waiting for something bad to happen.'

Troy nodded. He likewise could feel the tension building around town. Expectations that Isaac Dooley would not stand by and allow his only son to face a murder charge hung in the fetid air. 'I can't deny that I'll be glad when word comes through that I can take the prisoner to Trinidad for the trial,' was his only comment as he splashed another belt of whiskey into a glass.

Since the shooting, Jimmy couldn't help noticing that his esteemed boss was hitting the bottle rather too frequently. But he deigned to make any comment. It was none of his business.

At that moment, a knock came on the door.

THREE

TOOTHLESS
TIN STAR

'Come in,' the lawman called out.

A one-legged ex-soldier called Stumpy Jugg Binns hobbled in. He worked for Linus Oakum, a rancher who owned a spread to the north of Aguilar. Jugg had been Captain Oakum's sergeant during the war, before he was wounded at the Battle of Gettysburg. Oakum felt a bounden duty to Binns when the old jasper came looking for a job following the cessation of hostilities. He had been the general handyman at the ranch ever since.

'The boss asked me to come tell you that he reckons some land grabbers are trying to poison our water hole.' The old dude was sweating. And his words came tumbling out somewhat uneasily. Troy put it down to the hard ride over from the Oakum ranch. 'The boys found a dead steer down there. He reckons if'n you come at once, we could catch them skunks red-handed before they try it again.'

Troy was on his feet in a moment. Here was his opportunity to do some real work instead of just sitting around with this trial hanging over him. It would help clear his head. Without any further consideration, he jumped to his feet. 'You look after the store while I'm gone, Jimmy.'

Suddenly the melancholic mood of the previous few days lifted from his shoulders. Once again he felt like his old self. Unfortunately he never stopped to consider the fact that Oakum and the mayor were best buddies. The rancher was also a member of the town council. If'n he had, the events that followed might well have turned out differently.

Stumpy Binns made an excuse about collecting supplies so as not to accompany the marshal on his mission. Yet another clue that was missed by the unsuspecting enforcement officer. The first he knew that something was amiss came when he reached the water hole only to find all the steers happily drinking their fill with no apparent ill effects.

A frown of puzzlement quickly resolved into a full-blown howl of anger that he had been duped, made a fool of. He ought to have cottoned to the fact that Linus Oakum would have no compunction when it came to supporting his friend's devious machinations.

Troy cursed his ineptitude more than anything else. These turkeys had made him look a hapless clown. The Oakum land was a good two hours' ride north-east of Aguilar. He had ridden hard to get there and his horse needed resting before the ride back to town. Another bout of impotent cursing burst forth. He had been well and truly suckered. And it was no doubt at the instigation of Isaac Dooley. With only a greenhorn young deputy in charge of the prisoner, he shuddered to think what he would encounter on his return to Aguilar.

It was a tired and decidedly uneasy lawman who finally entered the town limits later that day. On the surface all seemed calm and relaxed. A sceptical frown blossomed across the ribbed brow. Too blamed calm. Rather than witnessing folks going about their normal business, all he perceived were empty streets. As he jogged up the middle of the main drag, faces were spotted at windows before quickly disappearing from view.

At the jailhouse, he dismounted and hustled inside. Jimmy Finch was there. But of Sheb Dooley there was no sign. A stream of irreverent profanity issued from between the lawman's pursed lips. 'What happened here?' The scathing query hissed out sharp as a razor. He knew that Jimmy could not be held responsible, yet still he could not contain a biting accusation. 'Why did you let that bastard go free?'

Jimmy was full of apologies. 'They gave me no choice, Marshal.' He held up his copy of an official-looking document, all fancy scroll writing and boasting a large red seal.

'Who's they?' was the waspish retort.

'Mayor Dooley and three members of the council came across soon after you had left and handed this over, claiming it was an official release form.'

Troy snatched it off the youngster and perused the contents. So this was how the scheming rat had managed to secure his son's release. He stood over the boy fuming impotently while Jimmy continued, desperately trying to vindicate his actions.

'It's signed by five members of the town council.' He pointed to the signatures, one of which was Linus Oakum. 'The mayor said that he had the authority to make binding amendments to the existing law if special circumstances arose warranting such action.' The boy held up his arms to indicate he had been given no choice in the matter. 'Those were his very words. How could I dispute his claim? I'm only a part-time deputy.'

Jimmy was distraught, almost in tears. Troy knew the boy was not to blame. They had both been hood-winked. But the responsibility rested solely with him. 'I'm sorry for being so hard on you,' he apologized, laying a commiserating hand on the boy's trembling shoulder. 'You weren't at fault, Jimmy. It was such an almighty shock to find the prisoner had been released. Shook me to the core, I can tell you.'

'You don't blame me then?' the boy jabbered, much relieved that his actions and been judged to be unavoidable.

'Of course not,' Troy reassured the edgy young-ster. 'Faced with a deputation of town worthies bearing this piece of rubbish, you were given no choice.' He held the slick piece of parchment up to the light. 'Looks mighty impressive, don't it? But looks can be deceiving. The mayor clearly has more power than I gave him credit for.' He threw it down on the desk. 'But it'll take me a month at least to have it overturned by the authorities in Trinidad. Meanwhile the ruling stands. And that skunk is able to roam around free as a bird.'

It didn't take long for news to spread that Marshal Garrison was back in town. Troy kept a low profile for the rest of the day. He needed to consider his position and how best to handle this usurping of his authority. Dooley had clearly bought off various factions to achieve his clandestine ends which left the marshal in a dicey position. Any action that the conniving mayor judged to be against his interests could be nullified by a mere piece of paper.

The following day saw the lawman girding himself to face the town and anything that might be tossed his way. Only time and circumstance could dictate how things would turn out. Barely five minutes on the street and he was faced with the strutting figure of Sheb Dooley, backed up by his three cohorts.

The roughnecks were leaning nonchalantly against the pitch-pine front wall of the Pioneer saloon. Like a dog challenged by others of its breed, Troy's hackles rose. His cynical thoughts reached the obvious conclusion. They had been waiting for just this moment. Dooley levered himself into a challenging stance when he spotted the approaching lawman.

His lip curled into an arrogant smirk of derision. 'Well, if'n it ain't Mr Big Shot himself,' he scoffed, imbuing the mocking remark with as much disdain as possible. His buddies obligingly guffawed. 'Come to arrest me again, tin star?' More cynical laughter. 'I don't think that would be a very wise decision.'

'You won't get away with this, Dooley,' the marshal snapped back, struggling to contain a rebellious streak.

'Seems like I already have.' Dooley scratched a match on the wall and lit up a cigar. He casually blew a perfect ring towards the hovering lawman. 'You've had your teeth well and truly pulled, mister. And there ain't a damned thing you can do about it,' he cackled, pouring out the abusive slurs.

'What say we call this guy the Toothless Tinstar,' suggested Three-Fingered Dick, absently toying with the stumps on his left hand.

'Yep, Fingers, you got something there,' Dooley agreed, chuckling. 'I like it. Reckon you ought to go visit the dentist, Toothless, and have yourself measured for a new set of gnashers.'

Alone in the middle of the street watched by half the town, the insolent mirth bubbled over inside Troy Garrison's head. Others within the crowd had begun sniggering among themselves. Had his life come down to this? To be verbally insulted by some no-account who should be facing a murder charge?

All he could feel was a dark mist settling over him, an aching void in the pit of his stomach. Circumspection, careful deliberation, all those essential traits that made for a good peace officer were fading into oblivion. That rash temper, so long effectively tamed, was now raising its ugly head again. He could feel his skin tingling as the black mask of violence elbowed its way back to the fore.

He struggled to shake off the Devil's Curse. But he was now past the point of no return. This wasn't the kind of law he had sworn to uphold. It was all a sham, a charade posing as justice. His whole being screamed out to put that right. Sworn affidavits meant nothing anymore. Mere fancy words on paper. All that mattered now was settling a score. And there was only one way forward.

'Step down into the street, Dooley, and we'll settle this right now. Man to man. No hiding behind your pa's coat tails anymore. This is between you and me.' Troy fixed a challenging eye onto the brash hothead.

In the bat of a gnat's wing the babble of conversation on the main street had been stilled. Nobody moved. Even the sun chose that moment to shelter from the coming showdown behind a cloud. Aguilar held its collective breath.

Dooley's jaw dropped. This was not how it was supposed to be. He was the one in control here. That crushed has-been ought to have walked away in disgrace to lick his wounds.

Sheb Dooley was no fast-draw gunslinger. For too long he had depended on his father for protection. And like any shifty manipulator, guile and cunning had become his principal methods of attaining his own dubious ends. A slick tongue and threats from the higher authority invariably succeeded.

Now he was being called out in front of the whole town. Some quick thinking was needed to swing the situation back into his favour. 'Shoot me down and it'll be you sitting in a cell awaiting trial for murder, Garrison,' was the spirited reaction. 'Have you thought about that?' A cocky smirk broke across the braggart's warped features. 'Everyone knows you're a slick gun hand.' He held up his hands to indicate his refusal to be coerced into any rash manoeuvre. 'And there's a whole town that'll bear witness to that.'

'Draw, you damned blasted coward,' shouted the irate lawman, stepping forward. Even Troy Garrison in his current distraught situation balked at gunning down a man in cold blood. But he was on the very brink of being unable to stop himself. His hand moved to the ivory butt of his trusted .44 Colt.

That was the moment panic infiltrated Dooley's sidekicks. Chuck Ryker had always asserted that he could take the lawman in a fair fight. Although he had never actually summoned up the nerve to put his bravado into practice. He was standing to one side. Without uttering a word, he grabbed for his own pistol.

Troy spotted the sneaky move out the corner of his eye. Those spontaneous reactions that had saved him so often before now kicked in. He dropped to one knee, his own shooter lifting. A fluid swing and two shots blasted from the gun barrel.

Ryker crumpled under the fatal overdose of lead. Clutching hands grabbed a veranda upright before he slid to the floor. Immediately the marshal's gun swung to cover the other gunnies. But they were too dumbstruck by the sudden downing of their pard to consider any form of retaliation.

Mist-shrouded eyes flicked hither and thither as the lawman took in the full implications of what had just occurred. The incident had happened so fast that nobody was fully aware of what had actually caused the shooting.

Sheb Dooley now took full advantage of that uncertainty by appealing to the crowd. 'You all witnessed that,' he announced to one and all. 'I had no intention of causing a fight. Yet this man deliberately gunned down one of my pals to goad me into drawing against him. He's the killer here, and nobody else.'

The gunfire had attracted the attention of Isaac Dooley, who now made his presence felt. 'What's all the shooting about?' His beady eyes fastened onto the dead man before swinging to the man in the street. 'Is this your doing, Garrison?'

His son quickly butted in. 'We were just talking, Pa. Trying to sort out our differences. Then, plumb out of the blue, he drew his gun and shot poor old Chuck down in cold blood.'

This blatant distortion of the facts finally brought Troy out of his dazed state. 'That ain't true. The skunk tried to gun me down. I was only defending myself.'

'A likely story,' scoffed the irate mayor. 'You were trying to get things over before the trial because you knew my son was innocent.'

'That's a load of hogwash and you know it,' Troy protested. But his appeal fell on deaf ears. Eyes overflowing with condemnation drilled into him. Hostility filled the air. Like a rampant herd of buffalo, the crowd made to surge forward. Troy realized that this was no place to linger. The Colt panned across the gathered throng as he backed off.

A couple of shots pumped into the air held the incensed mob at bay.

'Don't nobody move,' the threatened man growled out. 'I still have two bullets left. The next man that moves gets one.' He snatched the once-revered star from his vest and tossed it into the street. 'If'n you people figure that you don't need a marshal, you can have this back,' he snapped. 'And don't anybody try to stop me leaving. This town has been taken over by the Devil in a sharp suit. And I want no part of it. From here on you critters are on your own.'

Before Dooley or any of his supporters could move, Troy Garrison quickly disappeared inside the jail. Young Deputy Finch had been on tenterhooks watching the ghastly scenario unfold in the street. He was as disturbed by the sudden reversal of fortunes as anyone. But his loyalty stayed with his supervisor. 'What do you want me to do, Marshal?' he asked, keeping a level head for one so young. 'Just say the word and I'll back your play to the hilt.'

'I ain't the marshal no more, Jimmy.' The boy looked at him, surprise registered on his lean face.

'But you could bring my horse round to the back of the jail. I don't want those jackals out there to see which way I'm headed. Stay here and I'm a dead man. And it'll probably be from a bullet in the back.'

'Where will you go?' came back the startled retort.

'Ain't certain of that myself. But it'll be as far from Aguilar as possible. That's for darned sure.' And with that terse response, he hurried upstairs to his quarters. There was only time to grab a gunny sack filled with trail rations that were always packed and ready for an emergency such as this. Moments later he was hustling out back where Jimmy had his horse ready.

They shook hands. 'Good luck, boy. My one piece of advice to you is don't accept the tin star should it be offered. As the law stands in this town, it's nought but a poison chalice.' And with that he spurred off. Already, the muted sound of orders being handed out for a posse to pursue the killer of Chuck Ryker could be heard on the main street.

'Stay right where you are, fella. And don't move a muscle.' The blunt command jerked Troy out of his pensive recollection of recent events. A shot immediately followed. Troy lurched to his feet and grabbed for the small derringer pointed his way. By some freak accident, the .38 bullet had missed him.

'What the hell are you playing at?' he rasped, grappling with the gambler for possession of the small shooter. 'Trying to rob me. Is that it, you devious skunk?'

'Hold up there!' Fairplay remonstrated, attempting to pull free. 'You've got this all wrong. Take a look to your right and you'll see what I mean.' Puzzled, Troy gingerly relaxed his hold and did as bidden. 'That critter was about to sink his fangs into your ass. Seems like I scotched his game in the nick of time. You should be beholden to me for saving your bacon.'

A full-grown diamond back lay writhing no more than a foot from where Troy had been sitting. The spine-tingling rattle of its tail bones faded along with the life force. The potential victim immediately backed off. He shuddered. 'I never did cotton to those varmints. They give me the creeps.' Somewhat embarrassed at his false accusation of treachery, Troy apologized. 'Guess I reacted a mite sharply. It took me by surprise, is all. My mind was so full of that double-dealing in Aguilar.'

'Glad to be of service,' Fairplay iterated, slotting the Derringer back into the hidden pocket of his jacket. He picked the dead snake up by its tail and flung it into the rocks. 'Not the kind of guest to invite for supper.' A silence descended over the camp before the gambler tentatively broached the subject of his companion's recent disclosure. 'Reckon you must have shaken those other varmints off'n your tail by now, Mr Garrison, seeing as how you've come this far south.'

Troy stared into the mesmerizing flames. The comment from Harold Fairplay brought him back to his reason for being here in the wilderness, sharing a meal with this itinerant gambler. 'Reckon so,' he said taking a sip of the coffee that had now gone cold. He grimaced, tossing the dregs aside and accepting a refill from his companion. 'They must have given up after I crossed the border into New Mexico.'

'That sure was some tale, buddy,' Fairplay remarked, topping off his own cup. 'Ain't heard the like before. A mayor concocting his own laws to save his kin from the hangman. There again, maybe I'd be prepared to do the same for a son of mine, if'n I had one that is, which I don't. Never been married neither. Sounds too much like hard work from what I've heard.'

Troy offered no rejoinder. He was still thinking about the abrupt change of circumstances that his life had taken. One day a respected lawman, the next forced onto the owlhooter trail through no fault of his own. It was a hard fact to swallow.

'I can't help pondering over how Aguilar will fare with a corrupt mayor like Isaac Dooley in charge.' His voiced opinion was accompanied by a brusque guffaw that lacked any hint of jollity. 'It'll only be a matter of time before word spreads and all manner of riff-raff head that way. May God help the innocents among them. Cos I sure won't be there to pick up the pieces. I'm done with that game.'

FOUR

CIMARRON

The two unlikely travelling companions paused at a break of trail where a sign board offered two choices – *Cimarron 2m* due south or *Eagle's Nest 15m* to the west. A pair of cactus wrens were perched atop the arrowed depiction. Neither place appeared to entice the feathered visitors. With a series of decisive tweets they flew off towards the eastern upthrust of Capulin Volcano.

'What do you reckon, buddy?' Harold Fairplay enquired of his laconic associate. They had been together now for three days living off scrawny rabbit stew, beef jerky and sourdough bread, the flour of which had now run out. As far as the gambler was concerned, there was no contest.

'Eagle's Nest means another night on the trail.' He shook his head. 'Don't know about you but I'm in need of some good vittles and a clean bed.'

Troy arrowed a sceptical look at his companion. 'I thought you didn't have two nickels to rub together?'

Fairplay tapped his saddle responding with a knowing wink. 'But I have this fine piece of tack. It belonged to my father before he so kindly passed it on to me.'

'Another winning hand, I suppose,' came back the bemused reply.

'You have it in a nutshell, my friend. Pa never did appreciate how good a teacher he had been until it was too late.' The gambler then turned his attention back to their current choice of routes. 'So are we agreed? Head for Cimarron?'

Troy was less than eager. 'According to my knowledge as an ex-lawman, that place has something of a reputation for bad ways. If'n you are willing to take that risk it's all right by me. But we could be asking for trouble.'

'A place with a reputation, you say.' Fairplay's jaunty manner indicated he was in no way put off by his companion's hesitation. 'To my knowledge as a dealer of the pasteboards, that spells Money with a capital M. I can't wait to persuade these alleged wastrels to make me a deposit.'

Troy shrugged. 'I hope for your sake they don't object. Just don't call on me to pick you up off'n the floor afterwards.' Without waiting for a reply he spurred ahead. There was no denying that he was likewise ready for some rest and relaxation.

*

Around the same time, three riders were entering Cimarron having rode in from the Oxbow Valley where they were running cattle. Their leader was a stocky jasper boasting a permanent leer on his coarse visage. His hat was pulled down low concealing a mean-eyed look that bore little in the way of humour. His two sidekicks were equally hard-faced. These guys were not your run-of-the-mill cowhands. They drew up outside the Wayfarer saloon and dismounted.

'I could sure use a drink after all that branding,' suggested an emaciated rannie with the appropriate handle of Stick Drago.

'I'm with you there,' agreed his pal Greasy Joe Grass. 'You OK with that, boss?' Both men looked to Buzz Moran for his say-so.

'We've earned it, boys,' Moran said, shouldering his way into the dim interior where he deliberately lowered his voice, adding, 'That's another thirty head of prime beef ready for market.'

Rustling was not something to be recklessly bandied around. He need not have worried. The tumult of men drinking and gambling effectively swallowed up the remark. Moran led the way over to the bar pushing aside anyone who stood in his way. Nobody objected. The hardcase was well known in Cimarron as a guy best left alone if you valued your health.

'Three whiskeys!' he rapped out, slapping the counter to attract the bartender's attention. 'And make sure it's the best stuff you serve us. We don't want that slop palmed off on these ignorant saps.'

'You fellas know full well that the Wayfarer always provides top class liquor to all its customers,' the barman protested, though not too forcibly. He then splashed out three measures. Leaning forward, he consciously lowered his voice so that only the three newcomers could hear. 'I have it on good authority, boys, that Jarvis McAllister of the Wishbone M has fifty calves waiting to be branded. They're out there now on his eastern range. But you'll have to be sharp. He's moving them to the holding pens in a couple of days.'

Moran nodded. 'We'll make sure they're branded all right. But not with the Wishbone mark.' A mirthless sneer was matched by equally sniggering agreement from his two sidekicks. Then in a more robust tone he declared, 'Much obliged for the drinks, Chalky. And keep the change.' He slid a wad of greenbacks across the bar that was far in excess of the regular bar price of whiskey.

White-haired Chalky Bell smiled his thanks, surreptitiously scooping the dough up. The whole shifty exchange had passed unnoticed. 'You boys, stay here,' Moran instructed his associates. 'I have some business to conduct at the bank.' He slung down the rest of his drink and headed for the door.

Outside, Garrison and Fairplay were tying up their horses. 'Reckon I owe you a drink, Harold, for saving my skin when that rattler got a bit too friendly,' Troy announced with a smirk. 'But first I need to buy in some fresh tobacco and papers.'

'I'll hold you to that. So don't be long,' the gambler

said, untying the pack strapped behind his saddle.

It was the King of Clubs stuck in his derby that immediately caught Moran's attention. His lip curled in a rictus of anger. A growl rumbled in his throat. He stepped down to confront the object of his wrath.

'Well if'n it ain't that two-bit tinhorn, Harold Fairplay.' The greeting was by no means one of pleasure at encountering an old buddy. 'Remember me? The name's Buzz Moran. We clashed in Alamagordo when you took my entire poke.'

The gambler studied the speaker with care before replying. 'I certainly have dealt a few hands in that town. But I don't recall you, sir.'

'Well you should, having cheated me out of five hundred bucks. Dealing from the bottom as I recall.' Moran ground his teeth while poking the gambler in the chest forcing him back. 'Pity I didn't cotton to your dirty trick until later. By then it was too late. You'd skipped town.' He grabbed hold of Fairplay's jacket, pulling the victim close until their snouts were almost touching. 'So you can pay me what's due right here and now.'

'Even if'n what you say is true, which I fervently dispute,' Fairplay replied with a supercilious tone, nose twitching from the rancid odour of bad breath, 'my bank balance is completely empty. As are my pockets. So no amount of threatening will get you anywhere.'

Moran snarled but nevertheless released his hold on the other man. 'In that case I'll take that saddle and tack on account. It looks to be worth a sight

45

more than the mangy nag what's carrying it.' He moved across to undo the cinch.

'I don't think so, buster.' The brusque confrontation was from Troy who had just emerged from the tobacconist's.

Moran swung to face the unwanted interloper. 'Butt out, mister. This ain't no concern of your'n.' He turned back to continue with his appropriation of the gambler's sole piece of valuable property.

'Well I'm making it my concern.' A heavy hand fell onto Moran's shoulder.

Without any prior warning, indicative of a veteran saloon brawler, the rustler shook off the restraining hand and swung on his boot heel. A right hook brushed the meddling interloper high on the head. Lower down on the jaw and Troy would have been removed from the contest. 'I told you to keep your nose out my business,' the braggart rasped, although somewhat irked to see his adversary still on his feet.

He stepped forward intent on finishing what he had started. A slicing follow-up was meant to do just that. But Troy had quickly recovered. He ducked as the swingeing haymaker whistled by overhead, knocking the attacker off balance. Troy moved in with a couple of hard belts into the guy's stomach.

Moran doubled over, allowing the rejuvenated victim to deliver a brutal upper cut sending the recipient tumbling to the ground. Troy grabbed him by the shirt hauling him upright. But Moran was not finished yet. He grabbed a handful of sand which he threw in his opponent's face. Troy staggered back rubbing his eyes.

A gleam of triumph saw the brawler reaching for his gun ready to finish this interfering lunkhead off once and for all. Harold Fairplay now opted to make his presence felt. 'Leave it, mister,' he snapped out, brandishing the small Derringer in the guy's face. 'This fella may be small but at such short range he'll blow a big hole in your head.'

Moran's hand froze. Discretion persuaded him to think better of testing the claim. The momentary breather had given Troy the opportunity to clear his vision. And he was hopping mad. A fair fight had suddenly turned dirty. His right arm shot out, the bunched fist connecting with Moran's exposed jaw. The rustler's head jerked back. Unsteady legs reeled drunkenly as he blundered back into his two side-kicks who had just emerged from the saloon on hearing the fracas outside.

They were all set to join in. But the .44 Colt Frontier clutched in the ex-lawman's hand was sufficient inducement to stay any rash action. Moran wiped a hand over his mashed lip, his open mouth gulping in air.

'Who in the name of blue blazes is this monkey?' Troy enquired of his pard.

'Don't know him from Adam,' Fairplay replied, keeping his own gun hand steady. 'But he reckons I cheated him out of five hundred bucks in Alamagordo.'

'He's called Buzz Moran,' someone in the watching crowd shouted out.

Troy scowled as he eyed the panting roughneck. 'Well he don't look like he ever owned that much dough in his whole life.'

'You're asking for trouble, mister, sticking your nose where it ain't wanted,' Moran snarled back, pushing himself away from his buddies. His bandanna dabbed at the blood dribbling from a mashed lip. 'He's a tinhorn all right. And I aim to get even with the skunk.'

'Not while I'm around,' came back the stark retort as Troy hunkered down ready to continue the fight. 'We can continue this argument right here and now when you're ready, ape man.'

Moran looked as if he was about to do just that. Then he hesitated. The icy glint in the stranger's gaze proved he would be no pushover as had already been demonstrated. Prudence easily won the day. So he was forced to content himself with hurling back a few threats of his own. 'Stick around, fella, and you'll soon find out that nobody gets the better of Buzz Moran.' He prodded a finger at his nemesis while allowing his two partners to pull him away.

'We don't forgive or forget easy when no-good parasites try muscling in on our patch,' Greasy Grass butted in with vigour, knowing that the heat had been taken out of the confrontation. It was clear that this stranger was no milksop and knew how to handle himself. 'You'd be well advised to keep riding.'

The three toughs then wandered away casting hostile glares over their shoulders. There were other saloons where they could mull over the recent set-to and decide how best to lift those calves from McAlister's Wishbone spread.

Troy quickly forgot about them as he dusted himself down and headed for the Wayfarer saloon. He needed that drink badly. Meanwhile Fairplay's attention had been diverted by a couple of jaspers examining his saddle. He was not slow in capitalizing on their interest.

'As you can see, gentlemen, this is a fine example of traditional Texas workmanship. It has been in my family for generations.' The slick patter soon had the potential buyers hooked. 'And those are real silver conchos gracing the skirt,' he continued. 'Truly a unique piece of equine tack. I only wish that I did not have to part with such a magnificent heirloom.' An exaggerated sigh of regret issued from between pursed lips.

'What are you asking for it?' one of the men enquired, giving the saddle an appreciative nod.

'Quality, sir, cannot be measured purely in terms of dollars,' the gambler replied, even though hard cash was his objective. 'But I would be willing to offer it up as my stake if you care to play a few hands of cards. Shall we say stud poker?'

A portly well-dressed man in a store-bought blue suit who had been watching the fracas came across to join the trio. He addressed Fairplay while the two potential buyers were considering his proposition. 'Who is that guy?' the man asked, nodding towards the disappearing figure. 'He sure seems like a tough *hombre*.'

'His name is Garrison. We're partners,' replied the gambler, somewhat irritated at the interruption in the vital negotiations.

'Where does he hail from?' the man persisted.

Sensing a potential sale of his tack in the offing, the gambler was eager to divest himself of this inquisitive snoop. 'I never ask a man where he's from, only where he's going. You want to know his business, go ask him yourself.' Then he deliberately turned his back on the nosy meddler. 'Well, gentlemen, what's it to be?'

The rebuffed man did not take offence. His thoughts were on the stranger and a proposition he intended putting the guy's way. Inside the saloon, Troy was hunched over a cold glass of beer when the gent approached. 'I'll have the same, Chalky,' he said, tossing a quarter onto the counter. 'That should pay for this gentleman's drink as well.' Troy did not look up as the man slid onto a seat beside him.

No words were spoken as both men sipped their drinks. It was the buyer who broke the silence. 'You sure handled yourself like a true professional out there, mister. I don't know your background, and I ain't prying. But we need a man like you in Cimarron to keep order.' The man held out a hand. 'The name is Shadrack Fondrille. I'm the mayor of Cimarron and I also manage the bank here. So what do you say? Will you take the job? It's good pay, fifty bucks a month, and comes with free accommodation.'

Troy gave the outstretched hand a laconic sneer then turned back to his drink without replying. This was Fondrille's second rebuff in as many minutes.

But he was in no way fazed.

'Cimarron is a town that's going places, Mr Garrison,' he pressed on, intent on securing this man's services. 'But we need a strong presence to keep a lid on the wild antics that a boom town attracts. Buzz Moran and his boys are just one faction. The marshal we had before decided there was more profit on the wrong side of the tracks and lit out. You look like a straight-up kind of guy. If'n it's more money you want, I'm willing to increase the remuneration to sixty dollars plus a share of all fines exacted. That's a very fair offer, isn't it?'

That was the moment Troy chose to make his response. 'I've been down this road before, Mr Mayor.' His regard frosted over as the face of Isaac Dooley impinged its odious image onto his mind's eye. 'And I swore after my last brush with phoney law-makers that their version is just a heap of words wrapped up in a fancy package. In my experience a man should stick with his own interpretation of the law and to hell with anything else. And that's what I intend to do.' He deliberately turned his back on the hovering bureaucrat. 'I'm obliged for the drink but prefer to be left in peace now to enjoy it.'

Fondrille sighed. He sensed that this guy was the man for the job. Unfortunately a tarnished past at the hands of unscrupulous officials appeared to have soured his opinion when it came to all elected authorities. 'I'm sorry you feel that way. If'n you change your mind, sir, I'll be over at the bank.'

FIVE

CHANGE OF HEART

The next few days did not appear to support the mayor's view that a strong presence of law and order was needed in Cimarron. There had been a few incidents that might have warranted the attention of a badge toter, but nothing to worry about. Only the usual high jinx of cowpokes letting off steam by riding up and down the street shooting off their six guns. So long as the bullets went high it didn't pose any danger. In fact, this town appeared rather sleepy.

Troy's travelling partner had quickly settled in as resident house gambler at the Wayfarer following an unsurprising win from the potential purchasers of his saddle. The item in question still resided on the gambler's own horse. And of Buzz Moran and his pals, there had been no further sign. Maybe they were all wind and hot air after all.

But was this merely the calm before the storm? A

subtle trick that fate played on a fella's mind to make him complacent. The intimation that all was not as it seemed occurred on the third day when a passerby remarked to the idling ex-lawman, 'Hey buddy, do you know who was killed in Lambert's last night?'

Troy shrugged. 'Who's Lambert?' he enquired.

The man was taken aback. 'You must be new in town not to know about that Hells-a-poppin' berg.' He went on to explain that Henri Lambert was a Frenchman who had opened the inn back in '72. He operated a no-holds barred principle which had netted him big profits at the expense of a few broken chairs and regular visits from the undertaker.

'Seems to be quiet at the moment,' Troy observed.

'Can't last long,' the well-informed jasper remarked with a knowing curl of the lip. 'You mark my words. The undertaker will be called by the end of the day.' And with that gloomy appraisal, the solemn-faced cynic proceeded on his way.

An hour later Troy was sitting on a bench outside Fat Alice's Frontier Diner where he had recently enjoyed one of the good lady's special lunches. A quiet smoke to finish off and then he would go enquire if'n the local freight haulier needed drivers. Having left Aguilar in a hurry, he was getting rather low on funds.

The stogie was barely alight when the sound of gunfire disturbed the tranquil ambience. Birds fluttered skywards in panic. But the noisy commotion did not originate from boisterous cowpokes letting off steam. Angry shouts saw the sudden emergence of two men backing out of the Lambert Inn further down the street. Guns drawn, they began shooting at the swing doors as three more jaspers dashed out returning fire.

In the blink of an eye, the shooting had escalated into a full-blown gun battle. The protagonists ignored the threat to life and limb they were causing. Bystanders ran for cover as bullets zipped over their heads, smashing windows. A mother screamed grabbing up her youngster as a stray shot plucked at the sand inches from her feet. Troy joined the exodus from the street by hiding behind a stack of hay bales.

Dogs joined in the cacophony urging on the two factions, none of whom had thus far found a soft target. But such a situation could not continue without blood being spilled. And sure enough, moments later a cry of pain found one jasper in the middle of the street clutching at his stomach.

His partner carried on firing until his gun clicked on an empty chamber. He did, however, manage to wound one of the assailants. But four against two were poor odds and he curled over moments later, lying in the dust surrounded by a pool of his own blood.

A burly roughneck, smoking shooter clutched in his hand, walked up to the man who was holding his stomach. The wounded man sank to his knees as if praying for deliverance. And that's exactly what he received. Though not from the hand of God. A bullet removed half of his head. Without a flicker of remorse and cool as you please, his killer dispassionately blew the smoke from his gun barrel.

'Nobody insults my family name and walks away,' the killer snarled at the bloody corpse. 'You and your damned brother have been asking for trouble. And now you've had it in full measure.' His buddies nodded as they holstered their guns. The killer then laid a boot into the still form before returning to the saloon.

'Drinks are on me, folks,' he announced gruffly to a huge cheer. 'Those damn blasted Harker boys had that coming.'

'Now they've gotten their wish, eh Big Jake?' piped up one of the participants, addressing the instigator of the lethal fracas. The witty reflection elicited a raucous bout of hilarity.

'They sure as heck did, boys,' replied the man-mountain jovially. 'Line them drinks up, bartender. All that shooting gives a fella a mighty big thirst.' Regular patrons of the Lambert quickly emerged from cover and hustled across to the inn before the offer was withdrawn.

Others who were less inclined towards living in a war zone began to emerge from where they had been cowering. A couple of boys gingerly wandered over to examine the bodies. But most onlookers gave the gruesome sight a wide berth. One, however, made straight for the fallen men. An austere figure wearing a tall stovepipe hat complete with red sash and wearing a black drape jacket, this dude was clearly the local undertaker.

To prove the point, he began measuring up the corpses before nodding to a group of hangers-on who had suddenly appeared as if from nowhere. Some coins were exchanged. These guys knew the score as they lifted the bodies and followed the man in black down the street in a sedate procession.

Troy resumed his seat. Cimarron clearly had a much darker side than he had assumed. 'What did I tell you, mister?' his previous informant declared knowingly. 'And two for the price of one today.' The guy chuckled at his own witty riposte as he also joined the rush for free drinks.

Another man took his place at Troy's side. 'That big-mouthed critter who's buying the drinks is Jake Sprule,' a sullen voice declared. 'Him and his clan run a pig farm north of town in Colfax Draw. That feud between him and the Harkers has been simmering for months. I'm surprised it took so long to blow up.'

Troy turned to find Mayor Fondrille handing him a copy of the *Las Vegas Gazette*. The official jabbed a finger at a particular feature headed – *Everything is quiet in Cimarron. Nobody has been killed in three days.* 'This is yesterday's paper. The stagecoach driver gave it to me and it's out of date already as you have just observed.' Fondrille paused to allow the significance of the article to lodge in the other man's brain. 'Are you sure you can't be tempted to reconsider my proposition?'

The paper was idly tossed aside. 'What happens in Cimarron is none of my concern, Mayor.' His avowal was resolute. Nothing was going to sway him. 'I was planning on sticking around. All this incident has done is encouraged me to move on. I'm reckoning that Buzz Moran's advice is the best option on offer for a guy who values his health.'

Fondrille despondently shook his head. 'Guess I had you figured all wrong.'

'Guess you did at that.' Troy deliberately stood up and walked off. He had no intention of explaining himself any further. His days as a lawman were over.

Further down the street, he stopped to study the array of posters pinned up on the town noticeboard. One in particular drew his attention. A dodger offering a reward of five hundred dollars for the apprehension of one Pinky Blazer – also known as the Coffeeville Kid – for robbery and murder. A penned depiction of the baby-faced killer scowled back at him.

Troy sighed. Another young tough who thought he could challenge the world and come out smiling. Few of these brash kids ever made it into full adulthood. But that was their choice. A reflective cast passed over the craggy façade. He stroked his chin thoughtfully as another choice of career now presented itself to the ex-marshal.

He had never considered it before – Bounty Hunting. 'Now that might be a profession worth pursuing,' he muttered under his breath. And far more lucrative than badge-toting. He'd had dealings with those guys before. A breed of man who of necessity acted alone. But there was no denying, they sure lived well. A few years of that kind of life and a fella could retire. Provided, of course, he lived long enough.

Though with that mayor hovering in the background, he ought to continue south and seek out some potential marks elsewhere.

His decision was further endorsed the next day when a hulking gorilla sporting a heavy black beard stamped down the middle of the street. He stopped in front of The Happy Snapper Picture Gallery. The guy swayed as he pointed a twelve gauge shotgun at the store window. A garbled voice heavily charged with too much liquor brought Troy to the window of his room in the National Hotel.

'Ned Beatty, you in there?' The hulking bruiser didn't wait for a reply. 'Come out here right now, you shifty-eyed sonofabitch. Nobody takes Fred Miller's girl without his say so. And I ain't said so.' Without any further warning, Miller blasted both barrels of the lethal scatter gun. The window of the photography parlour exploded into a myriad fragments. Valuable cameras and equipment were destroyed in an instant.

Although liquored up, Miller had the wherewithal to reload his gun. He stepped up onto the boardwalk and pushed open the door. 'I'm coming in to get you, Beatty.' The rasping growl left nobody in any doubt that Fred Miller had death and destruction in mind.

Before he could enter the decimated premises, a girl ran up and tugged at his arm. 'Leave him be, Fred. It's over between us. Why can't you accept that?'

Miller shrugged off the girl's clutching hands.

'Nothing is over until I say so,' he snarled back. Maisie Gray recoiled under the impact of his whiskey-soured breath. Undaunted she continued with the struggle to drag him away. But Miller was past caring. One mighty heave sent her sprawling. Any concern for his ex-sweetheart's welfare was ignored as the angry braggart kicked open the door hollering all manner of lurid threats at the elusive photographer.

Eventually he emerged ranting and raving that the sneaky rat had fled. 'I saw the bastard at the end of Abbott Alley. The skunk was running for his life. But he was too far off to hit.' He staggered out into the middle of the street. The flailing shotgun was in danger of going off as he shouted out, 'I'll find you, Ned Beatty. And when I do you're a dead man. The only photos being taken then will be for the obituary column in the local news sheet.' Then he stumped off to drown his sorrows in the nearest saloon, which so happened to be the Lambert Inn.

Even with all this mayhem going on around him, still Troy Garrison tried to remain aloof. He had effectively convinced himself that any responsibility for law and order in Cimarron was not his affair. Although it was becoming harder to maintain an open mind. What happened later that day was the final straw that broke the camel's back.

Three roughnecks had emerged from another saloon called the Yellow Pig. They were clearly the worse for wear having been sampling the amber nectar within. The swaggering trio were jostling passersby, pushing them off the boardwalk into the

muddy thoroughfare. Nobody challenged the ruffi-
ans, merely glaring impotently at their backs.

A lawman's vigilant attention to detail immediately
sensed trouble brewing. The loudmouths were saun-
tering down towards where a woman was innocently
engaged in lifting various items into a wagon. Troy
felt his heart begin to pick up pace. It was clear
where this was leading. And his instincts were not at
fault.

The young hotheads began by hurling uncouth
remarks at the attractive girl. The unsettling incident
occurred right opposite to where Troy had
ensconced himself. He stiffened in his seat. The comments were less than respectful, more in the line of
cat house talk. He gritted his teeth hoping that the
varmints would depart when the lady paid them no
heed.

But her silence only served to inflame them all the
more. One grabbed an arm making her drop the
parcels. 'That ain't no way to treat fellas paying you a
compliment, missy. You should be more obliging,' he
slurred, draping his ungainly body over the cowering
girl.

'You tell her, Wes,' his pal said stepping forward,
eager to join in the fun. 'She sure is mighty perty,
ain't she Gad?' he said to the third man.

'Bulges in all the right places. Makes a fella go all
gooy inside.' The man called Gad pulled the girl
around and tried to plant a kiss on her lips.

That was when she cried out. Partly in fear, but
also in anger. 'Get your dirty hands off me,' she

protested, adding the weight of a flat hand to her dis-
sension. Gad was none too pleased that his impious
attentions had been repulsed so vehemently.

'Grab her, Hep!' he snarled out. 'This she-devil
needs teaching a lesson.'

Troy heard the loud crack from across the street
and knew exactly where this was heading. Suddenly
an unpleasant confrontation was turning nasty and
could only end in grief. He was left with no choice
but to intervene, adamant that any ensuing pain and
anguish would not be on the girl's side.

Tipping back the chair, he was across the street in
double-quick time just as the first man known as Hep
encircled the girl's waist in a bear hug. His aim was to
bundle her down an adjacent narrow passage. Troy
shivered at the prospect of what would await her if'n
these skunks succeeded in their dissolute intention.

He stopped ten feet from the group. 'You heard
what the lady said, scumbag.' The even-handed tone
was measured but held an icy bite. And it had the
desired effect. The three toughs paused, turning to
face this unwelcome intruder.

It was Gad Swiller who voiced the group's collective irritation. 'And who might you be, mister,
butting in on our fun?'

Hep laughed. 'Yeh fella, wait your turn like any
other decent asshole.'

Gad turned to resume what Troy had disturbed.
'Come on you guys, my pecker's getting itchy.'

'If'n I have to tell you again, this is going to end
badly for you.' The even tone had been raised to that

61

of a menacing command. 'Now you apologize like good boys and get about your business so this lady can do the same.'

Wes Garrity snarled. His baccy-stained teeth were bared in a rictus of hate. 'You're asking for big trouble tangling with us, ain't he boys?' The three men nodded, separating to face what was heading for a one-sided showdown. They hunkered down, hands flexing in anticipation of a fight they expected to win. Three-to-one odds were all in their favour.

'One last chance, boys, before Hell comes a-calling.'

Troy had not moved a muscle since first challenging the three young hellraisers. A smile loomed large and insolent as he waited for the inevitable. A rusty sign board creaked ominously as it swung to and fro in the light breeze. A cuckoo hooted before silence descended on the main street of Cimarron. Two dogs abandoned their pursuit of a cat to watch the action. And the town held its collective breath. All eyes were focussed on yet another confrontation from which only the undertaker profited.

'You've had your chance,' rasped Gad. 'Now grab your piece and get to shooting.' He didn't wait for his opponent to draw his weapon. None of the bums did. They all slapped leather at the same time.

But Troy was ready. His whole body was attuned to what needed to be done. And he had the distinct advantage of being sober. A thought flashed through his brain that most gunfights were precipitated by too much booze. And a sober man always held the edge.

His own gun was palmed in a trice, fanning the trigger. Three shots drilled into two of the hovering troublemakers. Wes Garrety clutched at his chest from which blood was pouring. It was a killing shot. The victim slid to the ground and stayed there. Gad was a mite luckier. He reeled back against the wagon causing the horses to snicker. It was only a shoulder wound but the casualty still posed a threat.

'Drop the gun, mister,' Troy hissed. 'Or the next bullet takes your head off.' The gun clattered on the boardwalk. His own weapon quickly swung to cover the third man whose hat was now lying in the street. Hep realized he was up against a professional gun-fighter. His arms lifted. At the same time he tossed the revolver aside. 'OK, mister, you win. I don't want no more trouble.'

The granite-hard look aimed his way displayed every sign that he would get just that if'n he moved a muscle. But Troy Garrison was now in full control. He stepped forward and helped the girl to her feet. Once it became palpable that bullets were about fly, she had dived behind the wagon.

His gun hand rock steady, Troy snapped out to the gaping Hep Charlton, 'Don't just stand there, bone-head.' The retort was cutting and decisive. 'This wagon needs loading up. But first you can make a full apology to the lady for your bad behaviour.' The wagging gun encouraged the deflated tough to stammer out a brief admission of guilt which the girl acknowledged with a curt nod of her head. Then she turned to face her saviour.

63

'I am much obliged to you, sir, for helping me out.' Her words sounded like a mountain stream trickling over shingle, cool and lilting. They perfectly matched the Titian locks of hair the girl casually brushed off her aquiline face. An action that was sheer poetry in motion. Troy was mesmerized.

He had courted a couple of women, both of whom had walked away considering the life of a lawman too dangerous a prospect. Neither matched up to this vision of loveliness now standing before him.

It took all of his self-control not to be entranced by the allure of this beauteous creature. But there was still serious work to be completed. 'Anybody would have done the same,' he burbled, forcing his gaze to keep the two surviving thugs under guard.

'But they didn't,' came back the grateful reply. 'Only you bothered to save a poor damsel in distress. And for that I am in your debt.' She scrambled up onto the wagon and swung it around. 'Thank you again.' Then she whipped up the horses and trotted off down the street.

Troy just stood there, tongue-tied. By the time his addled head had cleared, she had disappeared round a bend and was gone. He cursed himself for not even asking her name. Maybe he should ride after her. But the groaning of the wounded man and his shifty sidekick were a stark reminder that more urgent matters had to take priority. It was always the same, and doubtless always would be.

His vow to forsake the tin star had been wavering with each passing day he remained in Cimarron. Yet it was all he knew. And taking the job offered by Mayor Fondrille would enable him to stick around and perhaps become better acquainted with the mysterious female wagon driver.

'OK, fella, get this knucklehead down to the jailhouse.' Hep scowled while helping his buddy to shuffle off up the street, followed by Troy. 'The local sawbones can sort him out then the pair of you can cool your heels in the local hoosegow while I decide on your fate.'

It was only then that he realized he had automatically fallen back into his old role. And he was not the only one to have noticed that resumption.

SIX

A BABE IN ARMS?

Shadrack Fondrille had been observing the tough gunfighter's handling of the delicate situation involving April Prescott. Albeit from the safety of his office. Now the danger was past, he stepped out and quickly joined Troy as he escorted the prisoners up the street.

'That was a mighty impressive piece of work, Mr Garrison,' he extolled the instigator, keeping pace with him. 'Mighty impressive. I even go so far as to suggest it was the work of an experienced law officer.'

Troy made no comment. All he said was, 'Seeing as you're here, Mr Mayor, could you be good enough to direct me to the jailhouse?'

The mayor smiled to himself. He felt more upbeat than he had done in weeks. 'Straight ahead for two blocks then hang a right along Clayton Avenue.

66

You'll find it one block down on the left. And don't forget, there's living accommodation for the right man above the office.' He paused to allow his associate to mull over the implications before adding, 'Only if'n you're interested, of course.'

Still the laconic lawman refused to be drawn, maintaining a stiff back and a steady gun hand.

'And as a bonus,' Fondrille hurried on sensing his associate was wilting, 'the council could be persuaded to give fifty per cent of the reward money to a badge holder who arrests any wanted felons. And it so happens that Hep Charlton and his bunch have a dodger out on them for three hundred bucks apiece. That would make your share four-fifty. To show the town's appreciation of your actions today, we'll make it a round five hundred. Can't say fairer than that, can I?'

Now it was Troy's turn to smile. 'You're a smart dude, Mayor. I reckon you had this figured out all along.' Shadrack Fondrille struggled to maintain a deadpan expression. 'OK, guess you've gotten yourself a deal.'

The mayor clapped his hands, glad to relieve the tightness in his guts. 'When the doc comes to fix up Gad Swiller's shoulder, I'll have him witness your appointment.' He held out a hand. 'Welcome to Cimarron, Marshal Garrison. I trust it will be a fruitful alliance for us all.'

During his first week in the new job, Troy had little to occupy his time other than acquainting himself with the various factions operating in Cimarron. Most significant among these were the numerous saloons. News of the appointment had spread rapidly. It appeared that any hellraisers were lying low for the present to see how things panned out.

An edict was quickly passed, certified by the mayor, that all guns were to be deposited with the bartender while customers were inside their premises. As had previously been seen and experienced, too much hard liquor was the precursor of trouble. So men without firearms could slug it out if'n they had a grudge to settle. It was not a perfect solution by any means. Shooting could just as well occur outside on the street. But it was a start.

Troy had just left the Wayfarer where he had been checking up on Harold Fairplay. Although the gambler had made a good case for playing an honest game, the temptation was always there. And in a rough town like Cimarron, any shady practice that came to light was a death warrant for the perpetrator. So far, Fairplay appeared to have toed the line. There was no denying he was an adept manipulator of the pasteboards. A new suit and accommodation in the luxury suite at the National Hotel indicated his poor form in Branson had been effectively put out to pasture.

'Just so long as you don't become greedy,' the marshal made a point of warning his old travelling partner. 'A man gets used to the good things money can buy. And human nature as it is, there's always an itch to up the ante. That's when a man becomes careless.'

'I know my limits, Marshal,' the gambler assured his associate. 'Branson was a mistake. And I've learned from it.'

'Glad to hear it. But I'll keep reminding you.' Outside he wandered down to check on the next saloon, which also doubled as a theatre. The Silver Dollar was one of the most popular in town. It always featured a good main act which was changed every fortnight. But that was in the evening. During the day the chairs were cleared and the three-piece band provided music for dancing. Men could pay a fee for the privilege of tripping the boards with one of the professional hoofers.

He paused in the doorway. In contrast to the harsh brightness outside on the street, the interior of the Silver Dollar was gloomy. A quick look round, however, revealed numerous empty holsters. A nod of satisfaction that his order had been carried out elicited a smile of satisfaction. Just to make sure he then moseyed across to the bar ready to check with the bartender that all guns had indeed been handed in.

Before he was given the chance to speak, a grubby urchin suddenly appeared at his side. The kid tugged at his sleeve. 'A man down at the Lambert Inn said he wants to meet the new lawman.' The kid then took a step back before delivering the punch line. 'Reckons he's hungry and eats tin stars for breakfast.'

Troy gave the messenger a meaningful nod. 'Does he now? So what does this greedy critter look like?' he posited, fixing the kid with a look intended to scare the shit out of him. He succeeded. The boy's mouth opened and closed but nothing emerged. Troy bent down, his scowling face demanding a response. 'Out with it, boy, describe him to me.'

'He has smooth s-skin and c-curly blond hair. Don't look much older than me,' the kid stammered out, sweat bubbling on his dirt-sneaked face. 'B-but everybody's giving him a wide berth. And that gun on his hip sure don't look like its there for shooting rabbits. The barman didn't even ask him to hand it over.'

'Did he give you anything for delivering this message?'

The boy shook his head. 'He said you'd pay me.'

Troy laughed. This jasper sure had some gall. Nevertheless he tossed a dime into the air which was caught and pocketed before the kid ran off. So Pinkie Blazer was in town. It hadn't taken long for the word to spread that Cimarron had a new marshal. This was to be his first big test. Everyone would be watching to see how he handled the situation. 'Give me a drink, Rainbow.'

'A bit of Dutch courage, Marshal?' the man replied, pushing a shot glass across. 'You'll need it with a critter like Blazer. Rumour has it the kid needed a new gun when his old one fell apart due to all the notches he'd carved on it.'

Troy gave the comment a sceptical leer. 'I don't believe in rumours,' he replied with casual aplomb. 'In my experience they're usually spread to boost a reputation. Troublemakers like them are the ones who need to stiffen up their backbones, not me.' He tossed down the whiskey in a single gulp then turned around and headed for the door. And a date with destiny.

'Good luck, Marshal,' Rainbow Tupalo called out. Then in a whisper to another customer, added, 'The guy's gonna need it. That story ain't no daydream. I was running the Three Peaks saloon in Salida when the Kid gunned down Shifty Biglow. That was when he carved the third notch.'

'I heard that too,' the customer replied. 'And they say he keeps that gun as a memento.' The man levered himself off the bar. 'Reckon I'll go and watch the fun.'

The news that Pinky Blazer was gunning for the marshal was not received by other members of Tupalo's clientelle in the manner the barman had expected. 'Hear that?' gasped one startled drinker further along the bar. 'The Kid's in town and he's on the prod. I gotta see this.'

'Me too,' a couple of others agreed. Drinks were rapidly tossed down as the whole caboodle surged outside, eager to witness this historic confrontation. In no time the saloon was empty and the gossip was spreading through the town like wildfire.

Troy could sense the sudden change of mood around him. Expectant, keyed up. The Lambert Inn looked quiet enough as he warily approached the batwing doors. Slowly he pushed them open and quickly stepped inside, moving to the left into the shadows so as not to provide a clear target. It was a

71

long, narrow building with the bar stretching the whole length, a distance of at least twenty yards.

Only one man was stood at the far end hunched over a drink. He had his back to the door and was wearing a low slung cross-draw holster tied down in the manner favoured by gunslingers. It contained one of the latest Colt Peacemakers, pearl-handled without any notches. Pinky was clearly eager to change that. All the other drinkers knew the score and had fled the scene.

The only other person present was a twitchy barman who had been forced to serve the young hardcase. Sweat coated the poor guy's brow as he poured the Kid another shot. His hand shook, spilling half the contents on the counter.

'Guess you ain't heard about the new ruling in Cimarron, Pinky.' The remark cut through the tight atmosphere. 'I'm here to remind you. The wearing of guns inside all saloons is banned. And that especially applies to the Lambert Inn.'

Slowly the diminutive figure turned around. He looked just like his depiction on the poster. What had not come out in the pen drawing, however, was the icy regard, the look of pure evil emanating from the cherubic countenance. But what caught Troy's own studied gaze were the five shiny stars pinned to his vest. They could only have been acquired one way. It appeared that Pinky Blazer's grim reputation was no idle piece of fantasy.

'So you've done your duty, star packer. Now crawl away back where you came from so I can enjoy my drink in peace.'

The high-pitched nasal twang accorded with the Kid's youthful façade. Troy could readily imagine how Blazer must have been mercilessly picked on in his earlier youth. The perpetrators had clearly paid a high price for their ribaldry. It had left him with a huge chip on his shoulder. And those who wore the coveted badge were in his sights. Well that was about to end, one way or another.

The sneering rebuke was followed by a casual aside. 'Just drop the star on the table by the door when you leave. It'll make a fine extra piece of metal for my collection.' Then he turned back to resume his interrupted drinking as if the brief exchange was terminated.

The unhurried response that followed told him in no uncertain terms that it was far from that. Troy's tone had noticeably hardened. 'I'll tell you just once more, Pinky. Lay that hogleg on the counter and step away where I can see it.'

The baby-faced gunslinger lifted his round head and spoke to the petrified barman. 'This guy just don't listen, do he? You figure the big man is getting tired of life?' Hick Stoller just nodded in agreement before ducking down below the bar top. Blazer laughed. 'Something must have scared the beer puller. Now I wonder what that could be.' He then swung on his heel and in a single fluid motion, unseen by the naked eye, reached for his pistol.

Blink and you would have missed it. But Troy's concentration was honed to a sharp focus. He was ready for such a slick move having deliberately remained at the far end of the saloon, the limit of accuracy for the short-barrelled Peacemaker. With its extended barrel, his own Frontier had a more accurate range.

The two guns spat lead at one and the same moment. But the lawman had judged the distance correctly. Age and experience leapt to the fore. Pinky's bullet drilled a hole in the wall, more than a foot wide of the mark. Had he been closer, the odds would have been emphatically in the Kid's favour. But that was where a good lawman's guile and cunning came into play.

Troy's own chunk of lead was precise and on target. Blazer gripped his stomach attempting to staunch the flow of blood. A look of desolate surprise replaced the cold sneer. He reeled sideways clutching at the bar top, struggling to remain upright. The gun slipped from nerveless fingers. Not yet ready to give up the ghost, his left hand reached for a pocket pistol tucked inside his coat. A fatal move as two more slugs finished him off. Troy was taking no chances.

More to the point, he wanted the result of the showdown passed around town and beyond in order that all and sundry knew the score. Any troublemakers operating on his patch would be dealt with accordingly. The young thug slid to the floor, dead before his body lay still. Not since his formative years had such a serene countenance been seen on the puerile features. Troy walked across, his gun pointed unerringly at the still form.

'All right, Hick, you can come out now,' he muttered as the ashen-faced 'keep emerged from hiding. The new badge toter casually slotted the revolver back into its holster. He tapped the revered star. 'This piece of metal stays right where it is. And you best send for the undertaker.'

The marshal was given a wide berth as onlookers tentatively pushed their way into the Lambert Inn to view the renowned gunslinger's corpse. Even though death was no stranger to the saloon, eyes still popped in shocked amazement that he had been bested by this unknown tin star. A hush settled over the gathering throng as they absorbed what this meant for the 'anything goes' practice that had thus far prevailed in Cimarron's hottest drinking parlour.

'What's all this shooting about?' demanded a voice tainted with a foreign accent. Henri Lambert himself barged in through the back door, pushing all and sundry aside. The mordant complaint was instantly cut short as his beady peepers fastened onto the corpse. 'You been serving hard liquor to minors again, Hick?' he casually remarked to his barman with a slick guffaw.

It was the tall stranger standing alone in the middle of the room who provided the answer. 'Your place has been attracting the wrong type of customer.' Troy then stepped forward to confront the shifty saloon boss. 'Guess you can't have recognized the infamous Pinky Blazer. Well I'm giving you fair warning, *Monsieur.*' The saloon owner's title was accorded a mocking emphasis. A none too gentle finger prodded Lambert's chest. 'Things don't improve in this dump pronto, I might have to consider closing you down. Get my drift, Henri?'

For once, the garrulous Frenchman was lost for words.

'And the first thing you can do is collect in all the firearms from these jaspers.' And with that salient order, he headed for the door. A gap quickly opened to allow the tough-talking starman to depart. He paused in the doorway. 'You won't let me down will you . . . *Monsieur*?'

Outwardly having exhibited a stoically granite-faced persona, the facing-down of the young killer along with the Lambert Inn's ne'er-do-well clientele had left Troy in need of a strong drink to calm his nerves. Some guys regarded this part of the job as just another task to be completed. Others actually enjoyed it. Troy Garrison could never quite get used to the taking of a human life no matter how necessary that might be at the time.

The Coffeyville Kid had left him with little choice. Kill or crawl away like a licked mutt. So he had responded with the true grit expected from those who wore the revered lawman's badge. Reluctant though that action might have been. But when the chips were down, the response was forthright.

Before he had even turned down Clayton Avenue folks were casting wary glances at the tough lawman. A killing of this nature would already be on everyone's lips. Response to the standard question asked each morning in Cimarron as to '*Who was killed at the Lambert last night?*' would be received with eye-bulging astonishment today as the answer came back . . . Pinky Blazer!

SEVEN

WEB OF DECEPTION

Troy had been seated at his desk no more than ten minutes when the mayor bustled in. He was not alone. The recently cracked bottle of whiskey was deftly slid out of sight. The official's presence so soon after the showdown with Pinky Blazer, he would rather have postponed. But ever the consummate professional a forced smile greeted the intruders. 'What can I do for you gents?' was the buoyant welcome.

Mayor Fondrille was accompanied by a heavily moustached jasper with long grey hair poking from beneath the sugar-loaf Texas sombrero. Leather chaps covering bowed legs testified to a lifetime in the saddle. Straight away, the marshal pinned him down as a rancher.

'This is Jarvis MacAllister,' the mayor said, introducing the weathered fifty-something whose handshake was as firm as his granite façade. 'We've just heard about your set-to with Blazer. It's all over town how you bested him good and proper. Congratulations, Marshal.' The official looked at his associate. 'Sure looks like we picked the right man for the job, Jarvis.'

The older man nodded in agreement. 'Well done, Marshal. That young tough has been on the prod for too long. We can do without thugs like that around here.' McAllister spoke in a broad Scottish lilt.

The mayor then got down to business. 'Jarvis is a good friend of mine and he's having trouble with rustlers.'

'I've been over here this last twenty years,' the rancher said, answering the marshal's quizzical lift of the eyebrows. 'When my parents died, I decided to seek my fortune in the new world. Never regretted it for one minute. But this rustling is sticking in my craw, I can tell you. Those calves were prime beef stock and bound for the army post at Fort Union after they'd been fattened up and branded with my Wishbone M mark.' He lifted his arms in exasperation. 'Then they just upped and disappeared from the east range.'

'And it's not only the Wishbone,' Fondrille said, picking up the account. 'Other ranchers have also reported stock being stolen too.'

'My bet is on Moran and his bunch being the culprits,' McAllister bristled angrily. 'It's only since those critters arrived in the valley that we've had this problem.'

Troy immediately buckled on his gunbelt. That drink would have to wait. 'I'll ride out there straight away and nose around. See what I can find out.' He settled his new Stetson firmly atop the thatch of black hair. 'Rest assured, Mr McAllister. I'll get to the bottom of this.'

'Much obliged, Marshal,' the relieved man intoned.

Two hours later, Troy found himself crossing a rolling grass-covered expanse ideal for cattle grazing. It was interspersed with ranges of hills split by innumerable valleys. This was bunch-grass country that gave a blue tinge to the landscape. Herds of buffalo foraged contentedly as he passed. Their large woolly heads turned to study the passing traveller before returning to more important matters.

Soon after, he was riding along an elevated spur when he spotted a large herd down in the valley below. According to the signboard he had just passed he was now on Oxbow range owned by Chad and April Prescott. Troy drew to a halt, a suspicious frown clouding his leathery features as he studied the herd. McAllister had said that the Prescotts only ran a couple of hundred head.

This needed investigating. He was about to ride down and take a look when a bullet lifted the hat from his head. 'Stay right where you are, mister,' a familiar if rather crusty voice demanded. 'Now step down off'n your horse. If'n you can read, you'll have seen that this is private land.'

The marshal slowly complied. 'Not exactly the welcome I expected for a guy who recently helped you out, Miss Prescott,' he said, ambling across to where the woman had appeared from behind a tree. 'And I only bought this hat yesterday.' He stuck a finger through the hole.

'Sorry about that.' The girl apologized, lowering her rifle. 'I didn't recognize you, Mr Garrison.' Then her mouth opened in surprise as the afternoon sun glinted on the tin star. 'I see that it's Marshal Garrison now. Shadrack Fondrille must have been mighty persuasive. You didn't seem the type to stick around in one place for long. I took you for a guy with itchy feet.'

'Maybe I've found a reason to settle down.'

'And what might that be?' A coy smile lit up the girl's face.

Troy's heart skipped a beat. He was almost tempted to forget why he had ventured onto the Oxbow spread. Then he recalled his reason for being here and shook off the mesmeric allure quickly. There was work to be done. His face assumed the formal regard reserved for official business.

'Seems like there's a heap more cattle down there than a ranch this size can handle,' he asserted, firmly endeavouring to imbue an efficient tone into the remark. 'As there's been some rustling reported, I'd like to inspect your stock.'

Before the bewildered woman could respond she

was joined by a young man, who had to be her brother Chad, and three other hard-faced men led by none other than Buzz Moran. 'It ain't no business of your'n how many steers I run, Marshal,' Chad Prescott replied.

'It is if'n I think they're carrying a false brand.'

'Some of those are my beasts,' Moran declared with a sneer. 'I've brought them in from the Panhandle. No law against that is there?'

'Not if'n the brand has been registered.' He paused, holding Moran's arrogant gaze. 'And a running iron hasn't been used on the others.'

Moran stepped forward. 'You accusing me of rustling?' His fists bunched, eager for a re-match. 'Maybe we should finish what was started in town right now.'

'Some other time, Moran,' was the clipped rejoinder. 'Right now I've gotten more important things to do, like checking out that herd.' He turned about to return to his horse.

But Moran blocked his path. 'You're a legal man, Marshal. You should know that a warrant is needed to search a man's private property. Ain't that so, Chad?'

'Yeh, let's see that warrant, Marshal,' the young rancher stipulated, egged on by his conniving associate. 'Nobody examines stock on Oxbow land without good reason. And my bet is that you're just guessing.'

Troy's face hardened. His gaze narrowed as he pinned the four men down. 'I reckon you boys have something to hide. I'll get that warrant. Then I'm

82

coming back. We'll soon find out who's in the right, or the wrong. I know where my bet's going to be placed.' Pushing past the scowling hardcase, he mounted up tipping his holed hat to April Prescott. 'A pity this meeting had to end on a sour note, ma'am.'

A worried frown marred the girl's dazzling features. Instantly she regretted having presented such excessive aloofness to this handsome newcomer who had helped her out of a tight spot. Doubts impinged on her thoughts as she watched him ride away.

'That fella is gonna cause us trouble.' Greasy Grass was expressing the concern that was also in Buzz Moran's thoughts. 'D'yuh reckon we ought to ensure that warrant gets shot through with holes, Buzz?'

'Just what I was thinking,' concurred the gang leader. 'And not just the warrant. That critter could do with his own hide being ventilated.'

'And the sooner the better,' cut in Stick Drago. 'Last thing we need is some snoop of a tin star poking his nose where it ain't wanted.'

But Chad Prescott was less than eager to ally himself to murder. 'I allowed you fellas to bring stolen beef onto Oxbow land but I don't want no part of any killing, especially a lawman. That's inviting a noose around our necks.'

'Listen up good, kid,' Moran snarled, jabbing a finger into Chad's chest. 'You're in this up to the hilt and don't you forget it. We go down for rustling, and you come right along with us. And what happens to that perty sister of your'n if'n you're stuck in the pokey? She'll be left all on her ownsome. Do you want that?' He didn't wait for a response. 'There's only one way out if'n that's what you're pushing for. Until then, you do as you're darned well told. Savvy?'

Chad knew what he meant. That three grand he had borrowed from Moran still needed repaying. He was looking decidedly glum knowing he was indeed stuck in a slippery hole, seemingly with no way out.

Recognizing that he had the upper hand, Moran eased back. He slapped Chad on the back. 'Don't look so down in the mouth, kid.' A leery grin attempted to allay the young rancher's qualms. 'Ain't we all doing well out of this caper so far? The army pays good money for prime beef. And we have the perfect hideout here in the Oxbow to fatten 'em up and slap on our own brand. No sense in throwing all that away. Another year of this and we can all put our feet up.'

The three rustlers then walked away. Moran's thoughts were centred on how best to get rid of that interfering marshal. A critter like that could put the kibosh on his plans.

Unknown to the rustlers who thought she had returned to the ranch house, April had overheard the stark warning from Moran. She now confronted her brother about his involvement in the illicit deal. 'I knew there was something underhanded about those skunks. But I never figured you were in so deep.' The accusation was blunt and hard-hitting. 'Has my own brother resorted to being a common thief consorting with riff-raff like that?' She turned away to hide her distress. Tears etched a cheerless trail down the smooth cheeks. 'What would Ma and Pa have said?'

Their parents had both been taken by a severe bout of fever the previous year. The two siblings had been left to run the spread. But it was hard going. The big ranches were acquiring all the best deals leaving small-fry like the Oxbow with the scraps. As the man left in charge, Chad had soon come up against the severe challenges facing them.

The arrival of Buzz Moran and his offer had provided a lifeline; a chance to turn their fortunes around he could not turn down. Only later did he become aware of the consequences. By then it was too late. Chad had found himself caught up in a web of deception. He placed a hand on the girl's trembling shoulder. 'It'll be all right, Sis. You'll see. Those steers will fetch a good price from the army.'

April spun round, her face a mask of anguish mixed with sorrow. 'How can it be all right to break the law,' she espoused, pouring out a spirited rebuttal of her brother's illicit involvement with Moran. 'The Oxbow might not be in the big league, but we've done all right so far. We don't need Moran and his bunch of rustlers. I can't understand how you became involved with him in the first place. And now he's threatening to kill the new marshal.'

He brushed off the rustler's threat as mere bravado. But his sister's naïve assumption that extrication from the lawless endeavour was that simple brought a mirthless cackle from the young rancher's puckered lips. 'I kept it from you until now hoping things would pan out right. But that nosey marshal has put paid to that.'

'What do you mean?' asked a puzzled April Prescott.

'How do you think I managed to keep up the payments on this place? Money to mend the barn and bring in good breeding stock don't grow on trees.'

'So where did it come from?' the girl retorted.

Chad paused knowing his answer would not be well received. But there was no getting past it now. 'I borrowed three thousand dollars off Moran. The only way we can get him off'n our backs is to pay him back. I can only do that by going along with the rustling.'

April was shocked. 'There has to be some other way,' she insisted vehemently. 'Go into town tomorrow and see if'n the bank will extend our credit.'

Chad was less than enthusiastic. 'I'll do my best,' he sighed. 'But I ain't holding out much hope.'

While the Prescotts were struggling with how to disentangle themselves from the knotty mess into which they had become ensnared, Buzz Moran also had a thorny issue that needed resolving. His first order was for Drago and Greasy Grass. 'You two get back to The Kingdom and make sure the rest of them calves have our brand on their hides. Put the Oxbow mark on a dozen or so to keep Prescott happy. No need for him to know we're creaming off the bulk of the stock.'

'What a piece of good fortune that was, us coming

across The Kingdom. Everyone else round here reck-oned that hidden valley was just a legend,' Greasy Grass enthused. 'Only existed in people's minds.'

'You're right there, Joe,' Moran concurred. 'No damned snooper will ever find 'em up there in a month of Sundays.' His final order was for two more of his men to accompany him back to Cimarron. 'But I ain't taking no chances. That lawdog don't seem the type to give up easily. His big mistake was tan-gling with Buzz Moran. He don't know it yet, boys. But Cimarron will be minus another tin star by the end of the day.'

Hearty guffaws greeted this welcome announce-ment. It was a heavy-set jasper called Tubb Shelley who advocated what they were all thinking. 'We've gotten a good thing going here and don't want nobody upsetting the applecart.'

His pal Delano nodded his agreement. 'This is the best caper we've been involved with. You sure are one smart dude, boss.'

Moran preened, acknowledging the compliment with a superior smirk. 'Stick with me, boys, and things can only get better.'

But it was his sidekick Drago who cut to the chase. 'What about the kid?' he said warily. 'He's becoming too darned awkward for my liking. Reckon we should take him out as well?'

Moran spurned the suggestion. 'He still owes me a heap of dough. And I aim to collect. As long as he's in my debt, the kid ain't going to kick up a fuss. Blowing the whistle on our lucrative enterprise will find him on the same chain gang as us. He won't like that.' He rubbed his hands in anticipation of the forthcoming action. 'Enough jawing, boys. We've got work to do.'

EIGHT

NO EASY TARGET

After Chad had wandered off to consider the thorny issue of getting Buzz Moran off his back, April saddled her horse and headed back to Cimarron. The marshal had to be warned about Moran's murderous intentions towards him.

The man in question had arrived back in Cimarron and gone directly to the council office to apply for that all-important search warrant. He knew it would take some time to arrive. Back in his office a plethora of matters needed his attention. Minor infringements of the law were left in the hands of the local officer on the spot to deal with otherwise the system would grind to a halt. Only major crimes such as armed robbery and murder were decided by court action.

So it was left to Troy to collect the fine exacted from a sheep farmer who had allowed his animals to trespass onto the adjoining cattle spread. In normal circumstances, sheep and cattle on the same range spelled big trouble. But in Colfax County, the two factions had thus far managed to avoid any serious conflict. Troy had every intention of ensuring that situation continued. Swift action was accordingly required when a complaint was made by either side.

'You make sure those woollie backs stay off'n Wishbone M land in future,' the marshal asserted firmly as he wrote out a receipt for the imposition. 'Next time I might not be there to stop your animals being shot out of hand. And McAllister would be well within his rights as well. You got off lucky this time.'

'Much obliged, Marshal, we are very sorry,' the Swedish herdsman apologized in a thick accent while bobbing his head. 'It will not happen again.'

As the man backed out of the office, a far more welcome visitor arrived. Instantly the sheepherder was forgotten as Troy lurched to his feet and ushered the girl to a seat. 'This is a pleasant surprise, Miss Prescott. I didn't expect to see you again so soon after our last rather unfortunate meeting.' He pushed a finger through the holed hat. 'Although I am beginning to get rather attached to this hole. It gives me something to talk about on my rounds.'

'This is not a social call, Marshal,' the girl declared somewhat haughtily. The brusque putdown instantly wiped the smile off the lawman's face. 'I'm here to warn you that Moran and his cronies are planning to ambush you. I thought it only fair to come and let you know in person.'

'Well I much appreciate that.'

'I was also hoping that you might go easy on Chad.' The girl's aloof demeanour had thawed as she nervously played with her own hat. 'It's not his fault that he's become involved with Moran. The skunk has turned his head by lending him money he can't pay back. The man has him over a barrel.'

Troy held up his hand. His own manner had measurably hardened. 'I've been hired to bring law and order to Cimarron and anybody who goes up against that will be dealt with in an appropriate manner. If'n your brother is innocent he'll have nothing to fear from me. But any breach and he'll be dealt with like any other felon. A lawman can't be seen to favour one faction over another.'

The girl drew herself up, her pretty nose twitching imperiously. 'If that's the way you feel, there is nothing more to be said.' And with that she stamped out of the office much to the lawman's dismay. Although in his heart he wanted to rush out and apologize for the stubborn rebuff, he made a point of staying in his seat. Where the law was concerned, Troy Garrison was steadfast and resolute. It was the only way. Surrender to a pretty face and there was no knowing where it would end.

He sighed. It was better for all concerned that any prospect of a liaison of an amorous nature he had harboured should be squashed. Duty had to come first. Regretfully he pushed the notion to the back of his mind, instead toying with a pack of wanted dodgers that had recently been delivered. But his mind still lingered on the delectable contours of his latest visitor. April Prescott sure was one feisty dame. But that made her all the more intriguing.

Had he bothered to peruse the list of wanted felons, a worrying surprise would have been forthcoming. Instead he stuck them in a drawer to gather dust and went out with the intention of visiting a miner who had been threatened by claim jumpers. Hoping not to encounter the redoubtable Miss Prescott, he cautiously opened the door and peered out. Thankfully the lady in question was nowhere to be seen.

He quickly mounted up and swung his horse in the direction of the mine working. The sooner he sorted matters of this nature out the better. His mind was also alert to the warning passed on by the Prescott girl. Sharp eyes probed every inch of the landscape as he nudged the bay towards the edge of town.

'He's just left the marshal's office,' Moran hissed to his two associates. 'You get yourself up onto that water tower, Delano. Me and Tubb will hunker down behind this old shack for back-up.' He scoffed at the notion. 'Although I'm figuring you can't miss from up there. Just keep your head down so's he don't spot you.'

But that was exactly what happened. If Troy had not been forewarned of the impending ambush, he would have missed eyeballing the head ducking down behind the upper rim of the wooden tower. It was only momentary as the bushwhacker waited for his target to pass by below. Blink and he would have missed it. The rider deliberately kept close in to the ungainly structure forcing his hidden adversary to lean out over the lip above to sight his target.

He passed beneath where Delano was concealed, waiting until he judged the moment right. Then he dived off his horse behind a broken-down fence. That was the moment Delano fired. Too late the bullet zipped past Troy's head, ploughing a furrow in the sand a foot to his left.

The Winchester already palmed, Troy leaned round the edge of the fence and snapped off a couple of well-aimed shots at the startled villain. Surprise registered on Delano's face as he took both hunks of lead in the neck. His dead body slumped over the edge of the tower and hung there like a drying carcass of beef.

Moran cursed. This guy was proving to be a far more dangerous antagonist than he had bargained for. 'You go that way,' he hissed at Shelley. 'We'll catch the rat in a crossfire when he shows himself.' The two men split up, each sidling around the shack intending to trap their elusive prey in a pincer movement.

But Troy had quickly cottoned to the fact that Delano would not have been acting alone. He scrambled back towards some low hummocks of reedy sand. Crawling through the tall clumps of buffalo grass, he managed to reach an abandoned hut where he crouched behind an empty water barrel. Ears attuned to the slightest sound, he soon picked up movement around the side of the old shack on the far side of the trail.

A head gingerly showed itself. It was attached to a stocky frame holding a revolver. The man was looking towards where Troy's horse was casually grazing. But of the marshal there was no sign.

'You looking for me, buddy?' Troy growled in a sibilant whisper. Shelley's back stiffened. 'Toss that gun away, pronto. Then step out into the open.' For a good ten seconds neither man moved. The terse order was repeated. 'You heard me, fella. Drop the gun.'

The stocky rustler was about to comply when another shot rang out. A puff of smoke from the far side of the shack heralded the arrival of death. But Moran had made the same mistake as Pinky Blazer by misjudging the distance. For the second time in as many days, Troy's hat was lifted from his head. He felt the singe as the bullet whistled by.

He instantly returned fire forcing Moran to duck out of sight. The distraction had given Tubb Shelley the chance to gather his wits and make his own contribution to the melee. He triggered off two shots. But his target had disappeared. Moments later a bare-headed lawman appeared at a window inside the hut. This time there was no warning. A single bullet took the bushwhacker in the chest.

Two down, one to go. 'Your skulking pal has bit the dust, fella,' Troy called out keeping his head down. 'Best you come out now or join him in Hades.'

Moran knew the game was up. This guy had more lives than a cat. It was a relief that Garrison had not seen the instigator of the ambush. Time to disappear. Another occasion would present itself to finish the job properly. He pumped a final couple of shots at the hut to keep the guy's head down before backing off.

A heavy silence followed the cessation of hostilities. Troy waited a full minute before gingerly emerging from the hut. Gun cocked and ready, he hustled across to the other shack and kicked in the door. The weapon panned across the gloomy interior. But it was empty. A final check around revealed the remaining bushwhacker had vamoosed. The saving grace was that he had taken down two of the rats. Both were unknown to him. There was every reason to suppose that Moran was behind the ambush. But without any supporting evidence, an arrest for attempted murder could not be upheld.

Now it was the reluctant tin star's turn to cuss at the law that kept his hands tied. Grasping hold of a booted leg with each hand, he hauled the pair of corpses back into the middle of the main street and dumped them. A gaping crowd surrounded the gruesome sight.

Only one man was smiling. 'Another couple to be measured up,' Ezra Gloop, the undertaker breezily announced. 'You sure are a busy guy, Marshal. Not that I'm complaining. A fella has to make a living.' The tape measure immediately went to work, accompanied by a jaunty if tuneless bout of whistling.

The lawman did not share the undertaker's elation. It was only due to April Prescott's timely forewarning that he was still in the land of the living. He owed her. But that didn't detract from the unpleasant fact that her kin was involved with rustlers.

Back inside the office, he pulled open the draw of his desk and extracted the bottle of whiskey. After

what he'd just been through, a hefty slug was defi-
nitely warranted.

Buzz Moran needed time to settle his nerves. What
should have been an easy task had turned into a
nightmare. He was lucky to have escaped unscathed.
Just as important was the fact that he had not been
eyeballed. Pushing his horse to the gallop, he didn't
stop until he had returned to the hidden valley
known as The Kingdom where he and the remaining
members of the gang were holed up.

He was not in the best of moods as he dragged his
lathered mount to a halt and stamped into the cabin.
'You boys not finished that branding yet?' he rapped
out. 'What in thunder have you been doing?'

'Ironhand and the boys are on with it now,' Greasy
Grass replied.

Moran's face was a livid purple. He was not listening. His mouth screwed into a warped twist of anger.
Stick Drago looked warily at his partner. He immediately cottoned to the fact that the ambush had not
gone according to plan. The absence of Tubb Shelley
and Delano was a clear enough pointer. But he
remained silent. This was not the moment to make
enquiries. He left it for Moran to grudgingly outline
the grim events.

The rustler boss slouched in a chair. 'That skunk is
gonna pay dear for this,' he snarled out, snatching
the whiskey bottle and imbibing a hefty slug.
Although at that moment, how such an ambition
would be achieved was in the lap of the gods. 'You

guys make sure these steers are taken out the valley pronto before that nosey tin star comes sniffing around. I'm going over to Grumpy Gopher's trading post to arrange another sale.'

His next order was for his closest partner, Stick Drago. They had rode together since Moran saved him from a lynching after the inept rustler had been caught in possession of a running iron. 'You're in charge while I'm away.'

'You can count on me, Buzz. We'll ship 'em out to Fort Union by the back trail at first light.' In truth, Moran wanted to drown his sorrows and work out how to get his hands on the Oxbow. A few noggins at the trading post on the far side of Spanish Flats would help focus his devious mind. Not to mention assuaging his damaged pride.

He set out early the next day after ensuring the branded calves were on the trail. A four-hour ride brought him to the remote trading post by mid-morning. Two horses were already tethered outside. Moran paid them no heed. He was more than ready for that top notch moonshine for which Gopher Pete was renowned. He might be a miserable old grouch, but there was no denying the quality of his liquor. It was the main reason the trading post had survived for so long in this barren wilderness.

Moran hustled inside. 'A bottle of your finest, Pete,' he called out even before the door had closed.

The prairie dog lookalike laid his bulging peepers onto the newcomer. 'Ain't seen you around for a spell, Buzz,' he commented, lifting a jug and glass

97

from the back shelf. 'How's business these days?' With other ears flapping inside the single room, mention of the kind of business was deliberately omitted.

Moran never noticed the two men sitting at a table shovelling plates of bacon and beans down their gullets. He proceeded to bend the trading post owner's ear with his latest problem. One more vital reason for Grumpy's place being a hangout for ne'er-do-wells and owlhooters was his discretion. He was a sympathetic listener offering a safe retreat for those on the run. For a price, naturally.

'There's a new tin star operating in Cimarron,' Moran grumbled, sinking a large measure of the stiff brew. 'A real tough cookie. I have me a good deal going in the Oxbow Valley. But that skunk is threatening to upset the whole shebang.'

'This guy gotten a name?' asked Grumpy.

'Some guy who just drifted into town.' Moran ignored the question, glowering into the glass of hooch. Resentment towards the object of his wrath was rapidly coming to the boil as he outlined the consequence of the new lawman's arrival in the town. 'He even took down Pinky Blazer cool as you please. But I aim to cut Mr Troy Garrison down to size. No way will that goon spoil my pitch.'

Mention of the lawman's name brought startled looks to the faces of the two strangers. They immediately paused, knives and forks hovering over their plates. 'Hear that, buddy?' Sheb Dooley hissed, nudging his pard. The food was forgotten. Three-Fingered Dick Blezzard nodded as both men listened in. 'Never figured we'd come across that sneaky bastard again.' His eyes glittered with malice. 'This could be our lucky day.'

Blezzard was somewhat wary of his partner's sudden dynamism. Like the guy at the bar said, Garrison had proved to be a tough jasper. And he had clearly not lost his touch. But Sheb was already on his feet. He had the bit between his teeth and nothing was going to sway him. 'Come on, buddy,' he said hungrily, 'With two guys down, this jigger needs our help. I ain't about to let a chance like this slip away.'

The two men had been forced to leave Aguilar in a hurry after their other pal Stringer had been given the revered tin star by Isaac Dooley. A job that Sheb had automatically expected would fall to him. A huge argument had followed when the mayor had been confronted. Harsh words had rapidly turned to violence. Dooley senior was left in a pool of his own blood.

The fugitives had disappeared into the wilderness of the Sangre de Cristo Mountains. But without any means of support, and hunger gnawing at their innards, they had been obliged to rob a stagecoach heading for Trinidad. It had netted a few dollars from the passengers but little else. And they had been forced to shoot the guard who had raised objections to their need for funds. Not exactly an auspicious start to a life on the run.

Here was being presented an opportunity to rectify that omission.

Dooley sidled over to the bar. He eyed the sullen rustler with interest. 'Me and my buddy couldn't help overhearing you grumbling about a new lawman.'

Moran looked up. His mouth twisted with umbrage. He stepped back, hand hovering above his gun with hostile meaning. 'A guy can get himself killed listening in to a private conflab. You sick of living, mister?'

Dooley held both his hands up to indicate no affront was intended. 'I didn't mean no offence. It's just that I've had dealings with this critter up in Colorado. He shot one of my buddies. We want to get even.' He paused to allow the other man to digest his proposal. 'Let us join up with you and we can all benefit.'

Moran allowed the tight muscles around his mouth to relax. He studied the other man carefully along with his three-fingered associate. 'You fellas ready to lend a hand re-distributing cattle?' he proposed, his mouth crinkling in a sly smirk. 'If'n you get my drift?'

'We sure are,' Dooley breezed with vigour. 'Especially if'n the deal includes taking out that scumbag of a tin star.'

'Guess I could do with another two hands. And you guys look the part.' Moran turned to address the proprietor. 'Get that bottle of best Scotch out, Grumpy.' Things were looking a sight better for the rustler king than a few minutes before.

NINE

WINNERS AND LOSERS

Troy Garrison was sitting in his office still pondering over the difficult situation relating to the Oxbow and its lovely co-owner. Surprisingly, nothing untoward had occurred since the double shooting on the edge of town. Of Moran there had been no sign. Kids throwing stones at passing wagons, and couple of drunken cowboys shooting at the moon were the limits of his bother.

It seemed that his blunt response to the attempted bushwhacking had struck home and the rabble-rousers were keeping a low profile. Even the Lambert Inn had quietened down following Pinky Blazer's funeral. The burial had been well attended, mostly by morbid voyeurs eager to see a noted villain put away.

Acquisition of the search warrant had taken longer than expected, the nearest certified attorney residing in Las Vegas. After two weeks it had finally been delivered by the county express rider. So now he could no longer postpone the official visit to the Oxbow ranch for the purpose of examining the herd. He picked up the warrant and sighed. Why did life have to be so full of pitfalls?

The one light on the horizon was that he would be able to see the delectable April Prescott again. Although under these circumstances any hope of a thawing in her attitude was pure speculation. He set the battered hat at a rakish angle on his head of thick black hair. Before leaving he made sure his revolver and Winchester were fully loaded. A routine essential for the continued good health of any badge toter worth his salt.

Unbeknown to the lawman, Chad Prescott had just arrived in Cimarron intent on somehow raising the money owed to Buzz Moran. He naïvely assumed that paying off the rustler would categorically terminate their dubious association.

Chad tied off his horse outside the Wayfarer saloon just as Shadrack Fondrille was passing. The rancher blocked his way and came straight to the point. 'I need a loan of three thousand dollars against my spread.' The bluntly divulged request took the mayor by surprise, enabling Chad to press his case. 'The place is doing pretty well and I could easily pay it off in six months. What do you say, Mr Fondrille?'

Having regained his composure, the mayor appraised the young rancher with a stern frown. Thumbs hooked into the pockets of his silk vest, the tight-lipped regard did not auger well. And so it proved. 'You still have to pay off the loan for that prize bull, Chad. And according to my information, the Oxbow is not exactly a booming concern at the present time as you claim.'

'I know we've had a lean spell,' Chad protested. 'But it takes patience for a ranch to grow. And I know the good times are just around the corner.'

The unflinching stare of the chary banker should have told him that it was a futile appeal. 'I'm sorry, Chad,' Fondrille declared unequivocally. 'But you are a bad risk. I can't be seen to favour people who can't pay their way. It's bad for business. Good day to you, sir.' And with that brusque rebuttal he walked away.

Chad was steaming. And what better place to assuage his anger than in the saloon. He stamped inside and over to the bar. 'Whiskey!' The scowling demand was met with a sceptical evaluation by Chalky Bell. 'I'll take that revolver off'n you first,' he replied holding out his hand. 'All guns to be surrendered inside saloons. That's the new ruling.'

Following his blunt snub by that pompous banker, the young hothead was not about to be ordered around by some hick barkeep. Chalky saw the glint of resistance in the kid's eye. 'No gun, no drink!' he said, engaging the kid's arrogant stare full on.

Chad was all set to meet the challenge in his own

bull-headed manner when a voice of reason inter-
vened. 'My advice is to do as he says, young man.'
The cogent piece of wisdom originated from across
the room where Harold Fairplay sat idly shuffling the
pasteboards while waiting for his next game. 'No
sense in bucking the law and ending up in the
hoosegow.' The gambler paused to ensure his advice
had been heeded. 'You look kind of down in the
mouth, mister. Why not step over here and play a few
hands of poker? I always find that concentrating the
mind on cards helps a guy to forget his problems for
a spell.'

The bluster seemed to go out of the young man,
like air from a deflating balloon. He shrugged and
handed over the old Army Remington cap and ball.
The shot of whiskey was downed in a single draught.
He pushed the glass across the bar together with a
silver dollar. The second went down the same way. All
he had left were a few dollars, just enough to buy the
supplies April had requested.

Chad was about to rebuff the gambler's offer.
Then thought better of it. 'Why not?' he mouthed in
a liquor-charged drawl. 'My luck has to change some-
time. Maybe you're the fella to help me out.' He
slumped into a chair opposite the gambler and
slapped the lean clump of dollar bills on the green
baize. 'OK, mister, deal the cards.'

The two had been playing for no more than five
minutes when Buzz Moran entered the saloon with
one of his principal henchmen. Losing Delano and
Shelley had shaken up the rustler gang boss. But

104

those two new guys he had taken on had settled into their roles well. He had left them in The Kingdom with orders to finish changing the brands of some new steers that had been illicitly commandeered from a spread north of McAllister's Wishbone land.

No further action had been taken following the failed elimination of Garrison so he was pretty sure the lawman had not spotted him. It looked like he was in the clear. Hence the current visit to Cimarron to test the waters.

The two men immediately eyeballed their naïve sap of a partner playing cards. Moran aimed a sneering look at the soused player. That was how the dumb cluck had been forced to borrow money in the first place. He nudged Stick Drago in the ribs. 'You'd think the kid had more sense.'

'Mixing it with a professional tin horn like Fairplay ain't gonna do his chances of paying you back much good,' Drago remarked.

Moran did not like that one little bit. He stalked across to the table. 'So this is how you spend my dough. Gambling's a mug's game, Prescott. You should know that by now.'

'Mind your own business, Moran,' the young rancher spat out. 'I ought never to have become involved with the likes of you. Stick around and you'll soon see how I'm gonna pay you back. Then I'll be done with you for good.' He turned away. 'Deal the cards, Fairplay, and let's play some more poker. Reckon I'm onto a winning streak today.' A harsh cackle broke across the kid's flushed visage.

Moran watched for a while then returned to the bar stroking his stubble-coated chin in thought. It was clear that the kid's luck was no better now than it had been when they had first met. 'You're right about him walking out of here with his pockets empty, Stick. And it gives me an idea.' He leaned across the bar. 'Is that the kid's gun?' he asked the barman. Bell nodded. 'Let me see it.' Ensuring nobody was watching, Moran slipped the weapon into Stick Drago's hand. 'I've gotten me an idea how to finish this business once and for all in our favour.'

The two schemers made sure to leave their own guns with the barman before moving to the end of the bar where Moran proceeded to outline his plan. Once his crony was aware of his part in the skulduggery, Moran wandered across to the game where young Prescott had just lost his final bet. 'Lady Luck don't seem to be favouring you today,' Fairplay said without any hint of regret as he clawed in his winnings. 'Another time and maybe it'll change.'

Chad scowled. He could say goodbye to those supplies he was meant to have bought. How could life get any worse? He was soon to find out.

'How about one more hand, Chad?' Moran suggested sitting down at the table. 'As the tin horn says, your luck is bound to change soon.' The leery smirk on his face was as cold as a mountain stream.

'What in tarnation am I gonna play with?' the morose rancher retorted, angrily levering himself out of his seat. 'I'm plumb cleaned out. Ain't got two nickels to rub together.'

'I'll make you a fresh deal,' Moran offered, keeping a straight face. 'One hand only.' Moran leaned forward ready to deliver the punch line. 'The Oxbow against that three grand. You win and the debt is cleared and I won't bother you again.' A probing gaze fastened onto the kid's quizzical look. 'But lose and I take over the Oxbow. I'm offering you a once in a lifetime chance to clear the slate. You'll never get a better opportunity than this. And to show there won't be any cheating, the tin horn can deal.'

Chad was perplexed. He didn't know which way to turn. One hand could solve all his problems. But what if'n he lost? How could he face April having thrown away everything? Moran sat back watching the kid closely as he mulled over the ramifications of the proposition. 'It's a fifty-fifty chance for both of us,' Moran murmured, planting the seed of self-destruction. 'You won't get a better offer. Or maybe you ain't gotten the guts to take that risk.'

The snide taunt did it. Chad squared his shoulders. 'OK, Moran. You're on,' he snarled back. 'You've just made the biggest mistake of your life.'

Moran ignored the toothless jibe. 'You guys hear that?' the brigand said to the saloon patrons who had gathered round to watch the bizarre event. 'You're all witnesses to the outcome of this game. OK, tin horn, deal the cards,' he snapped at Fairplay. 'And make sure mine are good. I can hardly wait to get my hands on that deed of ownership.'

Both men carefully examined their hands. The tight lines creasing Chad's face testified to the

107

tension bubbling beneath the surface. He slowly fanned the cards in his hand. The King of Hearts, then another, this time the King of Clubs. He gulped, barely able to maintain that deadpan look essential to any successful gambler as he thumbed the third card into view. Bulging eyes struggled to comprehend what he was seeing. Three Kings followed by an eight and a five. His twitching eyes lifted to the gambler who was watching him, stony faced.

Chad slapped the two non-entities down. 'I'll take two,' he said swallowing down the nervous inflection tickling his throat. Fairplay dealt the cards.

Unbeknown to the kid or Moran, the gambler had unobtrusively manipulated the cards in Chad's favour being well aware that the rustler was attempting some devious ploy. Following his initial altercation with the brigand on that first day in Cimarron, the gambler recalled how Moran was capable of any devious stunt.

Unfortunately Fairplay had no idea what dastardly scheme was afoot. Had he cottoned to Moran's terminal intent beforehand, the gambler would have run a mile. That option had now passed him by. He was in this to the finish.

'Give me three,' Moran rasped studying his opponent closely. It was clear that Prescott was holding a good hand. But the rustler was not worried. His eye flicked towards the curtained-off passage behind the kid's chair. A slight wavering of the heavy material told him all he needed to know.

The final play was about to be made when a loud

report blasted apart the tense atmosphere. Fairplay clutched at his chest. He staggered to his feet, total shock registering on his creased up visage. So this was the plan. Give the impression that the kid figured the gambler was cheating. That was his last thought as he sprawled across the table sending the cards flying every which way. It was a killing shot. Harold Fairplay had dealt his last hand.

All those avidly watching the game unthinkingly stepped back, crashing into one another, fearful of being in the firing line of more shots. In the melee that followed, Drago sidled round the edge of the curtain and unobtrusively dropped Chad's pistol beneath his chair. The kid was so stunned at what had occurred he never noticed the sly manoeuvre. Nor did anyone else. Before Chad was able to proclaim his innocence, Drago stepped up behind him and laid a lump of broken chair over the kid's head.

Troy Garrison was passing the Wayfarer when the shooting started. He immediately leapt out of the saddle and rushed into the frenetic chaos caused by the lethal confrontation. A couple of bullets drilled into the ceiling soon brought a semblance of order to the milling throng. 'What's this all about?' he shouted, pushing his way through the crowd. 'Step back and give me some room.'

Moran and Drago made themselves inconspicuous in amongst the crowd.

'The gambler has been shot and it looks like Chad Prescott is the killer,' announced the bartender, holding up the fallen gun. 'This is his revolver. He left it behind the bar with me when he came in. But he must have slyly palmed it when my back was turned. Him and Buzz Moran were playing a winner-takes-all hand of cards. Chad Prescott always was a sore loser.'

'Guess that's how it was, Marshal,' Moran added, stepping forward. 'I had me a good hand. Last thing I heard the kid say was that the tin horn was cheating. Prescott must have been planning this all along. Why else would he have retrieved his own gun? It would have been me next if'n my buddy hadn't slugged him.'

The marshal gave the speaker a sceptical look. 'Anybody else see anything?' he asked. Nobody spoke up. Such was the unexpected nature of the attack and ensuing confusion, none of those present could swear to what exactly had taken place. Although the worm planted by Moran had clearly taken hold.

'The kid must have known he was gonna lose and decided to lay the blame on Fairplay,' one handy voyeur declared much to Moran's delight.

Bell obtained a bucket of water and threw it over the alleged killer who spat and gurgled, shaking his head, unable to comprehend his predicament. Garrison roughly hauled him upright. 'You're under arrest, mister. Now get your ass over to the jailhouse pronto.' He was none too gentle as he propelled the inebriated kid towards the door of the saloon.

A sinister notion of *déjà vu* infected his thoughts. It was as if the fate of Montana Red was being resurrected here in Cimarron with Fairplay this time paying the ultimate price for ignoring his own premise regarding cards and a soused opponent.

'Wh-what in blue blazes is going on here?' Prescott burbled weakly. He was still suffering from the effects of the pistol whipping. 'I ain't killed nobody. It's all a set-up.'

But the protestation of innocence was received with ugly jeers from the crowd. And the arresting officer was none too sympathetic either. The butt of his shotgun slammed into Prescott's back. 'Cut the caterwauling and shift your goddamned ass,' the angry lawman snarled. 'If'n there's one thing a judge detests, it's a poor loser who shifts the blame on to others. You've booked yourself a prime spot on the gallows for this dumb play.'

Chad moaned. Yet still he continued to vehemently dispute the charge. 'It weren't me. I swear on Ma's grave. Moran is at the back of this. He's been after taking over the ranch all along. And now the skunk has gotten his wish.'

Despite himself, Troy was intrigued. 'What do you mean?'

'The game was a win-or-lose hand with the Oxbow up for grabs,' Chad espoused. 'I had a winning hand but it didn't seem to bother him one way or the other. Believe me, Marshal, Moran is the snake in the grass.'

The marshal remained tight-lipped as he digested this unsettling revelation. But he was not about to believe the word of this young tearaway without proof. 'All the evidence points your way, mister. And

111

don't deny you've been in cahoots with that skunk to sell on stolen cattle. Until any other evidence comes to light, you're the only suspect.' He pushed the hunched figure before him, although this time with rather less antagonism.

Inside the saloon, the grizzly incident was soon at the back of everybody's mind as glasses were filled. Moran winked at his sidekick behind the bar as the two owlhoots left the saloon.

'No rush for me to go collect my winnings, Stick.' Moran was cock-a-hoop that his wily plot had unfolded exactly as planned. It was an unwritten law of the West that anybody caught cheating at cards forfeits the game, and accordingly the pot, in this case the ranch. And Moran could call on a dozen witnesses to support his claim that the Oxbow was now in new ownership. 'Let's head back to The Kingdom and make sure old Ironhand has rebranded those new steers.'

He couldn't wait to brag about how he'd outfoxed Prescott.

TEN

DOUBLE TROUBLE

With young Prescott incarcerated in the jail for first degree murder, Troy could not afford to leave him alone while he went out to the Oxbow to deliver the unwholesome news to April Prescott. At the same time he had to present the search warrant to look over their herd. Both were unsettling tasks he was decidedly loath to tackle. But such is the lot of a peace officer. Difficult issues followed you around like a bad smell.

Before he could leave town, he went in search of the mayor to enquire if a temporary deputy could be appointed.

'The best I can manage is to have Buckeye Dawson hold the fort,' Fondrille reluctantly acquiesced after much prevaricating. 'He was forced to retire as marshal two years ago when his eyesight began to fail. The old timer wears spectacles now but he still reckons he could hold down the job. Buy him a drink and he'll talk your pants down with stories of all the villains he's put away.'

'I've heard about that guy,' Troy mused. 'A real hot shot in his day so they say. Before my time. He must be over sixty by now.' Troy was loathe to bring in some old has-been. But if that was all he could expect, then so be it. 'Where do I find this guy?' he asked reluctantly.

'Reckon at this time of day, he'll be propping up the bar in the Silver Dollar,' Fondrille replied. 'Tell him it's an official appointment. He'll jump at the chance to pin a badge on again. You'll make the old fella's day.'

The current marshal of Cimarron ambled down to the Silver Dollar. And sure enough, when Troy entered the bar, Buckeye was indeed regaling all and sundry about the time he had brought in Wild Jack Mather. Troy listened for a spell before interrupting the old timer's flow. The one-time lawman was stonewalled at being asked to resume his old job, albeit on a temporary basis. 'Maybe if'n all goes well, we could make it a permanent thing?' he babbled eagerly.

He may have been grey as a bank of storm clouds, his hair thin and straggly, but the guy held himself straight. And behind those wire-rimmed spectacles the wayward right eye that had given him his nickname was bright as a new pin. Troy could readily imagine how the one-time starpacker had cleaned up Durango in its early boom period. But that was then.

'One thing at a time, Buckeye,' he cautioned the excited oldster. 'You ain't no spring chicken anymore. Your job is to look after things while I'm out of town. That's all. Especially no visitors for the prisoner.' Troy fixed him with a stern look. 'And don't try any heroics. Just keep a lid on the place until I get back.'

'Sure thing, Marshal,' the old guy asserted, eyes blinking behind his specs. Already he was checking the load of his trusty .36 Navy Colt. 'I'll be the soul of discretion.'

Troy needed to hang around for a couple of days to ensure that Buckeye Dawson settled in and knew exactly what was expected of him. In truth he had been putting off the noxious job of visiting the Oxbow ranch and facing the wrath of April Prescott. But it could no longer be delayed. She had a right to know about her brother's predicament. And those suspect steers needed checking out before Moran could sell them on. Accordingly, he bade farewell to his new deputy and headed out of town to face an unknown future.

Around the same time Buzz Moran, accompanied by his two newest recruits and Stick Drago, was likewise headed in the same direction. He reined up in a copse of trees overlooking the Oxbow ranch house. 'You boys stay here,' Moran ordered the others. 'I'll only need you if'n those two Mexican hands return unexpectedly from the east range. I sent a message down early this morning that some of their steers had strayed onto Wishbone land. The Prescott gal will figure it was sent by McAllister. Those greasers ought to be gone all day. Clever, eh?'

'Can't fault you there, boss,' Dooley gushed, maintaining a straight face. 'It was our lucky day when we met up with you.'

The rustler arrogantly accepted the compliment. 'And once I'm bossing the whole valley, we'll make short work of that interfering tin star.'

Moran was already in possession of a deed of transfer, a legally binding document giving him possession of the Oxbow. All it needed was the appended signature of one of the current owners. He was prepared to forget about repayment of the three thousand dollar loan to April Prescott's brother if she signed the ranch over to him. It was clearly worth a lot more. After learning how Chad had supposedly gambled it away, he felt confident she would have no option but to comply.

'But first I have to erm ... persuade the lovely April down there to sign on the dotted line.' He smirked at the thought of what was to come. 'That's the bit I'm gonna enjoy almost as much as the transfer.'

Stick Drago joined in. 'Wish I was helping out. She sure is one perty dame.'

'All in good time, old buddy. I just need her to play ball.'

The two new men remained tight-lipped. Since joining up with Moran, Dooley had seen how things operated. Moran had a good thing going. But Sheb

Dooley had never been one for taking orders. He liked to be the one in charge.

It had become patently clear that the smug bastard enjoyed lording it over his underlings. Only Stick Drago and Greasy Grass were treated anything like equals. More and more, Dooley came to resent his own reduced status. Branding maverick calves and altering the marks on stolen cattle was not his idea of the good life. He should be the one dishing out the orders.

From the start he had been figuring out a plan of how to turn the tables on the bumptious knuckle-head so that he could become top dog. Only Drago and Grass posed any threat to a takeover bid. The others were merely hired hands. They would work for whomsoever paid their wages. The ideal opportunity to set the ball rolling had presented itself when Moran had ordered Dooley and his pard to accompany him to the Oxbow. And here was the prefect set-up to get rid of the first obstacle.

The previous night the two newcomers had discussed how best to effect Stick Drago's removal. In the event, Moran had made things easier than they could have planned themselves.

'I'm going down there now,' the rustler said. 'You boys keep a sharp eye open for those greasers.' He mounted up and moved out of the tree cover heading downhill towards the ranch buildings.

Dooley casually signalled for Three-Fingered Dick to move across to a position where he was behind the oblivious Drago. When his buddy was in position,

Dooley affected a churlish rasp as if was in charge, 'I'm going for a smoke behind those trees, Drago. Make sure you keep watch while I'm gone.'

Drago spun round to face him. A look of anger cloaked the lean outlaw's gaunt features. 'Who in hell's name are you to order me about?'

Dooley's face cracked in a wide grin. 'I'm the guy who's taking over this outfit. And you, Mr Drago, are surplus to requirements.' Hands on hips he stood square on, facing the stunned rustler who was momentarily lost for words.

When Drago reached for his pistol, Sheb Dooley made no move to defend himself. He didn't need to. Before the unwitting rustler could draw, Fingers jammed the lethal blade of a ten-inch Bowie knife into his exposed back. The point jutted out from his midriff. Teeth gritted, the killer twisted the blade, churning up the victim's innards before dragging it out.

Drago's mouth flapped open. But no sound emerged such was the sudden nature of his demise. He sank to his knees then keeled over. The killer's wintry leer matched that of his associate as he casually wiped the gore-smeared blade on the victim's shirt. The deadly pair of conspirators stood over the dead man. Not the slightest hint of remorse clouded their self-satisfied mugs.

'Now we await the return of our revered boss and give him the same treatment,' Dooley murmured, gratification oozing from every pore of his being. 'That turned out much easier than I could have expected.'

And things were about get a whole lot better down below.

Satisfied that nobody else was around, Moran wasted no time in stalking into the ranch house. April Prescott was indeed alone. Her face turned white on seeing the odious rustler's impromptu invasion of her home. Fear mixed with resentment made her hesitant as the intruder advanced into the room like he owned the place.

'How dare you burst in here like this?' she remonstrated, trying to imbue a measure of defiance into the objection. 'What do you want?'

Moran replied with a smile of which a rattlesnake would have approved. April was clad in stained dungarees and a shabby felt hat having only just finished cleaning out the hen hut. In Moran's eyes she still looked ravishing. He moved a step closer eager to conclude the main business and get down to sampling the bonus treat.

The vital document wafted in front of her face. 'Be a good girl and sign this,' he said. 'Then we can have some fun.'

A look of puzzled intrigue made the girl lose some of her fear. 'What is it?'

'Only a deed of transfer giving me full ownership of all Oxbow land.' The reply was given with all the casual dispassion of a licence to sell liquor.

April's eyes bulged. 'Why in thunder should I do that?' she bristled angrily. 'Get your mangy hide out of here before I call my hands to have you thrown out.'

119

The empty threat was greeted with a mirthless cackle. 'I think that might be difficult seeing as you sent them over to the east range.' April's shoulders drooped on realizing she had been hoodwinked. He then went on to outline the bet and how her brother was now residing in the Cimarron pokey for the murder of Harold Fairplay. 'He accused the tin horn of backing my play by dealing him bad cards.' Moran allowed the girl to digest the false implications of her brother's reckless action before adding, 'I was playing a legitimate hand. You know as well as anybody that it's an unwritten law of the West that a cheat always forfeits any bet agreed on. In this case we were playing for the ranch.'

'I don't believe you,' April asserted weakly. 'Chad would never have been so foolish.' Yet in her heart, she knew that her brother was especially vulnerable when it came to gambling. After all, that was the reason he had been forced to borrow that money from Moran in the first place. But would he have bet their whole future on the turn of a card? It didn't bear thinking on.

'The truth speaks for itself,' Moran snapped, irritated at the girl's headstrong stance. 'Next time you're in Cimarron, ask anyone. They'll tell you. Now let's get this over with.' He held out the document. 'Sign it!'

'No, I won't!' she replied with vigour. 'And nobody can make me.'

Moran moved quickly across the room and grabbed a hold of the girl. She screamed. A struggle ensued that was only curtailed when the door crashed open and a cutting invective brought a halt to the ugly scuffle. It was a voice that Buzz Moran knew well, to his apprehension.

'Take your dirty hands off'n her right now.' Marshal Garrison stood in the doorway. The reason for his unwholesome visit had been forgotten when he heard the scream coming from inside the house. It had to be April Prescott and she was in trouble. Immediately he assumed that Moran and his bunch were the cause. And he was right. Luckily the rustler was alone. Troy drew his gun and spat out a challenge. 'You've been wanting to settle our disagreement for some time, monkey man. Now's your chance.'

'Shuck your hardware first,' the rustler demanded, unbuckling his own rig which he handed to the girl. 'Now we'll see who runs this valley. And it ain't you, starman.'

A furious growl rumbled in the braggart's throat. He pushed the girl to one side and dived at his adversary. A desperate struggle ensued. April could only watch and pray that Troy Garrison came out the winner. Both men tumbled to the floor where they rolled over upsetting tables and chairs as each strove for the upper hand. Moran scrambled to his feet and grabbed a brass candlestick, which he swung at Troy's head. April screamed.

The lawman saw it coming and shifted to one side. The heavy bludgeon hammered into the wooden floor inches from his head. He rolled away and was on his feet in moments. A straight left to the chin followed by a right hook pitched Moran backwards. He was stunned but not enough to dampen his ardour to fix this meddler once and for all.

Luck chose that moment to smile on him. His hand brushed against a table knife which was immediately commandeered. The sharp blade stabbed out forcing Troy to back off. 'Now let's see who gets to enjoy the lovely April for supper.' A spine-tingling guffaw accompanied the repugnant intention as Moran tossed the knife from hand to hand. He was clearly an accomplished practitioner. 'She needs a real man, not some wet-assed fraud.'

A couple of feints were followed by an all-or-nothing lunge as Moran drove the knife at his opponent's stomach. Troy twisted to the right but felt a searing twinge as the razor edge struck gold. Fortunately it was only a nick. The attack threw Moran off balance. Troy grabbed his wrist and wrenched hard forcing the guy to drop the weapon. 'You ain't the only one familiar with cold steel, scumbag.'

A backward jab with his elbow struck the rustler full in the face, busting his nose. A yell of pain found Moran grovelling on the floor. Troy quickly secured him with the handcuffs he always carried. He was breathing hard. He stood over the browbeaten outlaw, scowling as he proclaimed him under arrest.

'Harassment, threatening behaviour and attacking a law officer will do for starters,' he declared triumphantly. 'Reckon I can rustle up some more charges when I have you safely locked up.' He smiled at the unintentional crack as he removed the search warrant from his pocket. 'This should be enough to put you away for a long spell after I've checked on the stock you've been moving.'

With any further threat from Buzz Moran having been effectively nullified, the lawman turned his attention to the grateful recipient of his intervention. Without uttering a word she fell into his arms. All of Troy's senses were tingling as he stroked the lustrous hair, murmuring soft endearments intended to assuage the girl's anguish.

Instead, it had the opposite effect. April's need for consolation following the ghastly assault by Buzz Moran had made her realize it was a reflexive action she instantly regretted. Her natural defences had been lowered. She immediately pulled away from this man who had arrested her brother for a murder of which she was convinced he was innocent.

'Don't try soft-soaping your way into my affections, Marshal,' she snapped out. 'I appreciate your help in dealing with this critter. But that don't alter the fact that you still think we are in league with the rustlers. To cap it all, you've arrested Chad for cheating at cards and then shooting the dealer.'

Moran couldn't suppress a blatant snigger at the lawman's discomfiture. The derisive mockery was ignored as Troy attempted to appease the irate female. But he soon realized there was no way he could mollify the heated outburst. It was clear from her immoveable stance that it was a forlorn hope. So he reverted to his usual reaction when the law had been breached. 'Your brother was caught red-handed with a gun that should have been handed in when he entered the Wayfarer. That gun killed the gambler. Until such time as other evidence to the contrary is discovered, he stays locked up.'

The obstinate pair faced each other, neither willing to give an inch. It was April who broke the tense atmosphere. 'Then I suggest you get back to that damned jailhouse and take this varmint with you,' she announced, squaring her shoulders and crossing her arms. Her head turned away indicating that as far as she was concerned, the matter was closed. In truth she did not want to show the distress this unsettling confrontation was having on her nerves.

Troy wasted no more time in fruitless talk. He dragged the half-conscious rustler to his feet and left without another word being spoken. Outside he silently cursed his ineptitude. Should he have offered her an olive branch, tried harder? Too late for regrets now. He needed to get this skunk back to Cimarron before he was missed by the rest of the gang.

ELEVEN

LUCK OF THE DEVIL

'Well what about that?' Dooley gushed on spotting Troy Garrison arriving at the ranch house. And judging by his sudden rush for the door, he had cottoned to the skulduggery taking place inside. 'This is gonna be good, Dick. Wish I was down there looking in on the action. Who do you figure will come out on top?'

'My bet is on Garrison,' his sidekick averred. 'That critter is one hard lump of shit. He'll wipe the floor with Moran.'

'Ain't too sure of that, buddy.' Dooley replied. 'But it don't matter none. We're the fellas who are gonna be running the show.' The two hidden watchers settled down to await developments. Ten minutes passed before the door opened and Garrison

125

emerged pushing his handcuffed prisoner roughly towards his horse. The two riders set off back in the direction of Cimarron.

'What did I tell you?' Blezzard gleefully scoffed. 'It proves that Moran don't deserve to be running this operation.'

'You're right there, pal.' A purposeful glint of trickery found Dooley smirking as another piece of strategy began to form inside his devious brain. He was positively drooling with anticipation at the thought of muscling in on Moran's operation. 'And this is our chance to rid the world of two obstacles in one go. But we need to be quick.' In a moment he was on his feet and hustling over to his horse.

'What's the plan, Sheb?' his partner enquired, joining him.

'We have to get ahead of them and set up an ambush,' Dooley extolled, spurring off. 'And the best place around here is at Black Tail Gap. We can cut across country and be ready when they pass through.'

The main trail back to Cimarron was designed for the easy passage of wagons. As a result it meandered around craggy buttresses and outcroppings taking a longer course than that followed by the two bush-whackers. Dooley leathered his cayuse to a full gallop. Both men tightened their hat fastenings as the wind whistled by, the broad brims flattening against ribbed foreheads. Zipping round clumps of cholla cacti and yucca, they were able to maintain a direct course.

Three-Fingered Dick struggled to keep pace with his long-term buddy. It had always been the same. Ever since they were kids. And later when Sheb had saved him from a sadistic bunch of five Comancheroes who were each intent on acquiring one of Dick Blezzard's fingers. And all because he had insulted their pride by having his way with one of their women.

Sheb had ridden into their camp all guns blazing and cut him free. But not before the gruesome torment had removed two digits. Admittedly, his pal was drunk as a skunk at the time. But that didn't alter Dick's eternal gratitude. He had been with the guy ever since. And doubtless would be until the end. Those fingers now graced Blezzard's hat. A grim reminder that he owed a lot to his buddy.

Branches of mesquite reached for their clothing as the pair of miscreants rode like the devil was on their tails. Such a frenetic tempo could only be held for a short period. The horses were tiring when Dooley veered back onto the main trail where it narrowed to form a rocky defile. Fractured turrets of sandstone searched for the bunching cotton bolls overhead. This was Black Tail Gap.

The two men led their snorting horses behind some boulders where they could not be spotted. And there they waited, each man keeping watch on either side of the trail. Ten minutes passed before the steady drumming of hoof beats signalled the arrival of their quarry.

Judging the moment right, Dooley spurred out

into the open. Revolver drawn and aimed unerringly at the lawman, he snapped out, 'Hold up there, starpacker. Raise your hands. Any move towards that hogleg will be your last.' Blezzard kept Garrison covered from the far side.

'I was wondering when you guys would show up,' Moran breezed.

'Where's Stick hiding himself?'

'He couldn't make it,' Dooley replied with a straight face. Moran responded with a puzzled frown. 'And this is where we part company as well, Buzz.' The gun shifted towards the cuffed rustler. 'Your days in this game are numbered. Me and my pard are taking over the reins.'

Before either the lawman or his prisoner knew what was happening, two shots blasted out, their harsh reports bouncing off the rock walls. Fountains of blood spurted from the lethal puncture wounds. Such was the brutal impact, the rustler was hurled out of the saddle.

That was the moment Troy Garrison recognized his assailant. 'Sheb Dooley!' For a moment he was thunderstruck, lost for words. 'How in the name of. . . ?'

Sheb laughed out loud, slapping his thigh. 'Gee, Marshal, you seem surprised to see me! A piece of good fortune, don't you think, me and Dick coming across that bungling no-account over at Grumpy Gopher's trading post?' Dooley was enjoying himself. 'And when Moran revealed the name of the local tin star, I knew my lucky star had come home. Life sure is smiling on old Sheb. Me taking over from Moran while at the same getting rid of an irritating burr like you.'

Troy made to lower his arms. Dooley stiffened. 'Don't try any funny business, asshole. I could have easily dropped you with a rifle. But I wanted the great Troy Garrison to see exactly who it was gunning him down.'

'You'll never get away with it,' Troy snarled, keeping his hands aloft. The shock of this unexpected encounter was beginning to fade. 'That treacherous rat of a father must have put you up to this.'

A scathing guffaw from the killer conveyed what he thought of that comment. 'Don't make me laugh, buster. He's like all the rest of them bums. Figured I didn't have the balls to stand up to him.' An ugly curl of the lip told a sinister finale to the story. 'He learned the hard way that nobody pushes Sheb Dooley around. Anyway, enough of this chinwag. We need to be getting back to The Kingdom. Now it's your turn to meet the Grim Reaper. And not before time neither.'

The killer's trigger finger tightened. And there was nothing Troy could do to prevent that unwelcome encounter.

Before the execution could be carried out, the throaty roar of rifle fire stayed his hand. Twin puffs of smoke some two hundred yards distant were coming from a nearby rise. The wide brimmed sombreros told Dooley that the two Mexican ranch hands were returning early from their wild goose chase. He railed impotently at their cussed interference. The fact that they were shooting from galloping horses was the only reason the shots had missed their target. Any closer and the two bushwhackers would have been buzzard bait.

Both men snapped off a couple of warning shots at the approaching riders even though they were well out of range. They had the desired effect of forcing the ranch hands to pull back. Dooley hollered out an impotent curse. 'You've had Lady Luck on your side far too long, Garrison. But she just turned sour.' He fired a bullet to finish off the lucky bastard, which plucked at the lawman's head, spinning him around. A second struck him in the chest. Caught in the open, there was no more time for any further delay if'n the two reprobates were to save themselves. But Dooley was satisfied his adversary had hit the high trail.

'Until we meet in Hell, tin star,' he sneered, swinging his cayuse around and urging it to flee in the opposite direction.

Moments later Manuel Rodriguez and his amigo, Sancho Villa arrived on the scene. Villa pumped a couple more shots at the fleeing desperadoes while his partner attended to the stricken marshal. He was lying on the ground unconscious. But a few dribbles of water from Villa's canteen soon brought him round. The Mexican vaquero carefully helped him to sit up.

'You very lucky, *señor*. Bullet hit star and ricochet

off,' Villa declared in a lyrical cadence. '*Cabeza* mighty tough. Ees only a flesh wound but leaking much blood.' He tied his bandanna around Troy's head to temporarily stem the flow. 'We take you back to ranch where lady *patron* can fix you up properly.'

Rodriguez helped the marshal back onto his horse commenting, 'Good for you, *señor*, we come along. You know those bad fellows?'

'We've met before,' Troy replied in his usual laconic manner, wincing as an angry barb lanced through his head. 'I'm obliged, *amigos*. They were the ones who sent you off on that turkey hunt.'

'We thought something fishy going on when Señor McAllister denied any knowledge of trespassing *ganado*,' Rodriguez explained. 'Rode back *mucho rapido* fearing *señorita* in danger.'

'You were right there,' Troy informed the two loyal hands. 'I caught Moran red-handed at the ranch trying to force Miss Prescott to sign over the ranch to him. We had a bust-up and I made an arrest. We were heading back to Cimarron when those bushwhackers butted in.'

'Why they shoot own *hombre*?' Sancho asked, clearly baffled by the strange course of events.

'It's a long story.' The wounded lawman was tiring rapidly from his wound. His head slumped as he gasped out, 'Some other time maybe.'

'Pardon, *señor*. Too much *conversacione*. We get you to ranch pronto.'

TWELVE

GOODBYE TO BUCKEYE

Spotting her two ranch hands escorting a hunched figure between them, April hurried outside. Even from a distance she instinctively knew that something bad had occurred. Her breath caught on noticing the blood-stained rag around Garrison's head. He was clearly in a serious way. Without any demand for explanations, she ordered the Mexicans to bring the wounded man inside.

'Lay him down on the sofa while I get hot water and bandages,' she said, her manner efficient yet caring. The time for clarification would be later when the man had regained his strength. He had clearly lost a lot of blood.

Half a dozen stitches were needed to sew up the

lacerated tear. A few belts of whiskey helped to nullify the pain. In Troy's mind, however, every jab of the needle was worth it just to have this vision of loveliness fussing over him like a mother hen. A wistful expression cast a spell over his ashen features while relishing the tender ministrations as she bandaged his head. All too soon she was finished. 'You will need to stay here a couple of days to regain your strength,' she murmured in a voice laced with concern.

There was no objection to that as he stared dewy-eyed into those limpid pools of nectar. 'Anything you say, ma'am,' he muttered. He was more than happy to have this girl attending to him for as long as possible. It was almost worth having been shot and left for dead.

But after three days, it was clear that he could not postpone the inevitable departure any longer. There was no knowing how things were panning out if Sheb Dooley had indeed managed to take over the rustling. He needed to get back to town and set about scotching their plans.

April had been fully apprised of all the events during his three-day sojourn at the Oxbow. Troy had even opened up about his ignominious departure from Aguilar along with Sheb Dooley's odious part in the affair. The two had become close, even though the grim prospect of her brother's future still cast a bleak shadow over their budding relationship.

'I'm sure in my mind now that Chad was framed by Moran so the rat could gain possession of the ranch. I just need to prove it,' Troy admitted after one of their heart-to-heart discussions. Breakfast was finished and he was reluctantly preparing to depart. 'Moran might be out of the picture, but things will be just the same if'n Dooley has taken over.' An edgy tension showed in the way he failed to meet her gaze.

'What's wrong, Troy? You seem worried.' His heart skipped a beat. This was the first time she had not addressed him formally. April Prescott's aloof manner towards the strong-willed lawman had considerably tempered since his near-death altercation at Black Tail Gap. Likewise, Troy's own unbending attitude.

He hesitated. Would she be willing to do what he wanted? There was only one way to find out. He breathed deeply. 'Would you be prepared to give evidence against the rustlers?' A nervous pause followed while he studied her reaction. 'I know Chad got himself involved because of Moran's conniving. And he may still have to face rustling charges. But I'll do what I can to sway the court in his favour.'

For a brief moment the girl's stiff bearing intimated a refusal to implicate her brother. Then she relaxed, a half smile playing across the sleek features. 'I have seen them changing the brands. It's been on my conscience ever since. The only reason I condoned it was in the hope that Chad would see sense. Anything that will stop those critters and give him a fresh start is all right with me.'

A relieved Troy Garrison bid her farewell. It was time to leave. He was saddling up prior to leaving the ranch when she came outside to see him off. 'I'll do all I can to prove he was framed for killing Fairplay,' he assured her.

April placed a hand on his arm as they stood side by side. Her touch sent a tingle rippling through his taut frame. 'I know that my brother is weak when it comes to money matters. But he's no killer. Chad is a good man. And so are you.' A squeeze of the hand elicited another yearning quiver. 'I'm coming along. I need to speak with Chad. I'll soon know if'n he's telling the truth.'

Troy had no objections. Anything that would prolong his contact with this girl was to be welcomed. His fervent hope was that he could successfully defeat the rustler gang, now more than ever due to the likelihood of it having fallen into the clutches of Sheb Dooley.

Following the shooting of Buzz Moran and the unforeseen interference of those two greasers, the bushwhackers had hightailed it back to the gang's hideout inside The Kingdom. Greasy Joe Grass had come out of the cabin to meet them. His hand rested on the butt of a holstered Remington Rider when he saw that only the pair of newcomers had returned. The look of suspicion clouding his gnarled visage gave ample warning that the rustler wanted answers.

His first question was blunt and to the point. 'Where are Buzz and Stick?'

The two new men had separated on approaching the cabin so as not to present an easy target when the inevitable confrontation took an ugly turn. Dooley affected an easy-going demeanour. 'They won't be coming back, Joe. We had a little trouble with that tin star.'

'What sort of trouble?'

'He hit the high trail,' Blezzard averred, grinning wolfishly.

'And so did your buddies,' Dooley added. 'Me and Fingers here decided this enterprise is too good for a lunkhead like Moran to be bossing.' He leaned over the neck of his horse. 'So we're taking over. You have any objection to that?'

'Don't matter none if'n you do,' Three-Fingered Dick interjected. 'It's a done deal.' Grass was given no chance to voice his clear dissent. Hot lead blasted him into the great beyond. Even before the dead man had hit the ground the insurgents dived off their mounts and took cover behind a nearby wall.

'Listen up good, you guys inside the cabin,' Dooley called out. 'Anybody agin us taking over this outfit can ride out now with no comeback.' He winked at his sidekick. The chances of that happening were nil. And the two rustlers inside the cabin knew it. 'So what's it to be, fellas? Extra bonuses for those beeves you've been working on, or . . .' He left the obvious corollary for their imaginations to mull over should resistance be their chosen option.

Moments later the door opened and a grizzled fifty-plus veteran hobbled out. Ironhand Joplin was certainly no mean-eyed hardcase. But there was no better man with a running iron. The old guy could change any brand into something even the most sceptical eye would fail to notice.

His associate was a simple-minded desperado called Fireball for obvious reasons. He had been caught in a prairie blaze when his horse tripped in a gopher hole. Only the quick witted reactions of his *compadre* had saved the guy. But the incident had left the young cowboy's face badly scarred. Sarcastic jeers from less sympathetic colleagues had resulted in gunplay that left three men dead, forcing Fireball onto the owlhooter trail. That had been five years before. Ironhand had felt it his bounded duty to look out for the tetchy kid ever since.

'We don't want no trouble, boss,' the old guy declared, keeping his hands raised. Dooley smiled. He liked that, being called 'boss'. It sounded good. 'Just so long as the dough keeps rolling in, we're both happy.'

'Glad to have you with us, boys,' he iterated, stepping out from cover. 'That was a smart move.' They went inside to celebrate the new association in time-honoured fashion with a jug of Grumpy Gopher's moonshine. So that was settled. But there was no time to lose. Dooley wanted to reach Cimarron to ensure his plan came to fruition.

The new boss left Ironhand to finish off the branding. Accompanied by Dick Blezzard and Fireball, Dooley wasted no further time in returning to Cimarron. His first call was to see Chalky Bell at the Wayfarer. With his two confederates backing his play, Dooley bluntly informed the crooked bartender that they were now in control of the operation.

'What happened to Moran and the others?' the 'keep nervously enquired.

'Never mind about them,' came back the snarled rejoinder. 'You in or out?'

Three guns pointing his way helped to make up Bell's mind double quick. Dooley then went on to explain his plan to bust Chad Prescott out of jail and take him back to The Kingdom to write out an official transfer signing over the ranch to him. 'Your job is to make sure the good citizens of Cimarron don't organize a posse. Once Prescott has signed on the dotted line, I'll send the critter to join Moran and Garrison stoking up the fiery furnace.'

Bell's eyes bulged with shock as the wagging pistol answered the question. 'You any beef with that?'

Things were moving a mite fast for the barman who was less than keen about putting his head above the parapet. He could back out but that option offered a one-way ticket to the graveyard. 'Guess not,' he muttered nervously. 'But how am I supposed to scotch a posse?'

'Use your initiative,' rasped the irritated new gang leader. 'Persuade them that a dead tin horn ain't no loss to the town. Anything. That's why I'm prepared to pay double the normal rake-off that Moran paid you.'

That soon brought Bell to heel. He nodded. 'Leave it to me, boss. I'll have them eating out of my hand.'

'Now get back behind that bar,' Dooley ordered. Exhilaration at the success of his devious scheme was showing in flushed features and the crisp delivery of instructions. Soon he would be the monarch around here, and this would be his kingdom. It felt good. 'When you hear the shooting, join the crowd at the jailhouse. Plant the seed that it must have been those two Mexican ranch hands who busted him out.' A jabbing finger pressed the barman's part in the subterfuge. 'Remember I need you to be convincing.'

The three gunman then hustled down the street and round to the back entrance of the jailhouse. 'Not a word until we're inside,' Dooley hissed, drawing his gun. Luckily the rear door was unlocked. Led by Dooley, they silently crept inside, cat-footing along a corridor to the main office. The sound of snoring could be heard through the closed door. Dooley smiled. This was going to be like shooting fish in a barrel. He burst through the door brandishing his shooter.

An old guy wearing spectacles grunted as he struggled to shrug off the soporific effects of his illicit doze. In his heyday Buckeye Dawson would never have been caught out like this. But he was well past his prime. Struggling to his feet, Dooley pushed him back down.

'Is this old coot all that Garrison could manage to guard the place?' he scoffed to his associates. 'A washed-out has-been who can't even see straight.'

Buckeye's gnarled features creased with indignation as he tried to recapture some of his old vigour. 'What's going on here? Who are you guys?' he blurted out, attempting to draw the old Navy Colt on his hip.

Dooley wasted no more time on idle blather. His gun butt slammed down onto the deputy's head. Out for the count, the once revered lawman slumped to the ground, blood pouring from a brutal scalp wound. Chad Prescott was immediately on his feet. His eyes glittered as the thought of freedom impinged on the morose ruminations that had been haunting his mind since the arrest. He had no idea who these jaspers were, and it didn't matter. Just so long as they unlocked the cell door. And that is exactly what happened.

'I don't know who you guys are, but I sure am glad to see you,' Chad gushed. It was the sinister follow-up that hinted all was not as it should be. The beaming smile disappeared from his youthful kisser. The assailant's next caustic remark only served to prove his ominous fears. Dooley snapped out an order to his heavily scarred partner in crime. 'Fireball, you haul this old hunk over beside the cell. We'll make it look as if the kid jumped him when his meal was delivered.'

It was now clear to Chad that he was jumping from the frying pan into the fire. Blezzard confirmed as much when he turned his revolver to cover the prisoner. 'We need you in one piece, Prescott,' he said. 'Moran handed in his resignation as boss of this outfit yesterday.' That comment brought a fit of ribald chuckling from Dooley. 'And my buddy here has taken over. So don't try any funny business.' It was now patently clear to Chad where this was leading. And it certainly boded ill for him.

Dooley then went on to demonstrate his ruthless determination by grabbing a holstered pistol lying on the desk. 'This your gun, kid?' Chad merely nodded dumbly as the gun was cocked and aimed at the unconscious deputy. Two deafening blasts echoed around the room. Blood mushroomed from the fatal bullet wounds in the guy's chest. Dooley then tossed the smoking weapon into the empty cell. 'OK, boys, let's go,' he averred with a satisfied grin.

Hustling their prisoner back down the corridor where they had left the horses, the group of riders quickly disappeared amidst the amalgam of back lots behind the main street. Moments later the mayor and a host of others entered the front office, only to find their deputy had been shot dead. Of the prisoner there was no sign.

The contrived course of events was soon espoused by the irate mayor. 'Looks like Prescott jumped old Buckeye, clubbed the poor fella down, then shot him.' He grabbed the discarded pistol. 'This is Prescott's revolver. He must have snatched it up when he escaped.' A growl of anger rippled through the rapidly growing crowd who were cramming into the small room.

'You reckon he could have had some help?' asked one bystander.

'Sure looks like it,' another guy concurred. 'But who would want to help Prescott? He shot down that gambler for cheating.'

'Could have been those greaser ranch hands from the Oxbow,' Mayor Fondrille butted in. 'They always were loyal to the Prescotts.'

Chalky could have hugged the guy. 'Anybody see which way they went?' he said. The crooked barman was at the front eager to display his apparent rage for the abhorrent act of cowardice. 'Only a coward would have gunned down a respected old timer like Buckeye Dawson. Chad Prescott needs stringing up.' More nods of accord and muttered imprecations greeted the barman's assertion.

At that moment, much to Chalky Bell's astonishment, Troy Garrison pushed his way into the room. April Prescott was close on his heels.

THIRTEEN

KINGDOM COME

Troy's eyes widened in shock as they fastened onto the very dead corpse of Buckeye Dawson. Things had moved on a sight faster than he could ever have anticipated. This had to be Dooley's work. He had clearly carried out his threat and was wasting no time in making his presence felt. And the critter must have abducted Chad Prescott for the purpose of securing that all important title deed signature to the Oxbow ranch.

Before he could speak, Mayor Fondrille put the hostile looks of those in the room into words. 'About time you showed up, Marshal. Where have you been while poor old Buckeye was trying to do your job?' Antagonistic grumbles supported the mayor's stance. The pompous official laid his cynical gaze on the lawman's associate and gave a perceptive nod. 'I think we can all see what you've been up to, can't we

143

boys?' More snarled grunts.

The situation was taking an ugly turn. Troy needed to assert his authority, and fast. 'You're talking a load of hogwash. I've been chasing after a ruthless desperado who has killed Buzz Moran and taken over his gang.' He paused to allow that startling development to sink in. 'It's him and his bunch who have busted Chad out of jail for their own devious ends. And I aim to go after him.' Without waiting he asked for volunteers to form a posse. 'Who's willing to come with me?'

The stunned silence that followed was broken by Chalky Bell who realized he needed to scupper that notion. 'We've only gotten your word for that,' the barman promulgated firmly. He pointed a finger at the blood-stained ex-deputy. 'Prescott tricked Buckeye then shot him. And you being in cahoots with this dame don't exactly put you in a good light, Garrison.' The implied accusation brought a flurry of growled agreements. 'I sure ain't putting my neck on the line for a blamed rustler like Chad Prescott. And all for shooting a tin horn gambler.'

Troy was all set to ram the accusation down Bell's throat when April chose to intervene. 'My brother had his faults but he's no killer,' she remonstrated, her chin jutting forward defiantly. 'He was forced to join up with Moran to save the ranch.'

'I've heard enough of these weak excuses,' the mayor interjected. 'This is your responsibility, Garrison. We're paying you more than the going rate to protect this town. So get to it sharpish and do your job.' And with that he stamped out of the jail followed by the other disobliging minions. Bell could barely conceal a satisfied smirk. But he would need to tell the new boss about Garrison's return from the dead.

The two crestfallen confederates were left in a quandary. April wandered disconsolately into the cell where her brother's hat and coat had been left. It looked as if he had been hastily bundled out. Her gaze narrowed on spotting a playing card poking out from beneath a plate. It had clearly been placed there deliberately. 'Over here, Troy,' she called out warily. 'What do you make of this?'

The marshal took hold of the King of Diamonds and frowned. Was it just a random card dropped mistakenly, or something having more significance? A King – perhaps it was a clue as to where he had been taken. Then a stirring thought struck him. 'Just before he gunned me down in Black Tail Gap, Sheb Dooley let slip they were headed back to The Kingdom. Does that mean anything to you?'

April's shapely brow creased in thought. 'It's a valley somewhere on the edge of our land where it merges with the Badlands. I've never been up there. Only Chad has any idea where it is. He went there with Moran sometimes. Apparently it was where they kept the stolen cattle before rebranding them. They call it The Kingdom.' She scratched her head. 'They never told me how to find it. All I know is that it lies somewhere to the north in the Blue Boar hills.'

'Looks like I'm going to have to do this the hard

way,' the lawman opined somewhat reluctantly. 'You head back to the ranch and wait for me there. Maybe those two Mexican hands know something. I'll ask about this Kingdom in the Wayfarer. And Chalky Bell better be co-operative or I'll run him in for obstruction.' He stuffed the evidence into his pocket and made to leave.

April rested a hand on his arm. 'Take care of yourself, Troy. There are too many bad guys out there. And bring Chad back safely,' the girl purred, fastening her big round eyes on this tall raw-boned stranger who had so recently entered her life. 'I'll be waiting.'

Her captivating smile, those big blue eyes inches away. It was all too much for the smitten marshal. This time he surrendered to the urge that had been gnawing at him ever since that first meeting on the street outside. Without a word, he held her close and kissed her on the lips. There was no resistance as both yielded to a passion neither wanted to end. But end it must. There was still danger ahead. And Troy Garrison would need all his guile and cunning to bring the culprits to justice.

He walked down the corridor and out the back door. His aim was to slip into the Wayfarer by the rear door to avoid any unwelcome comments about his competence. He silently entered a passageway at the end of which was a curtain near to where the killing of Harold Fairplay had taken place. Just before he pushed his way through into the main bar room, Troy noticed a shiny object on the floor. Intrigued, he reached down and picked it up.

It was a cigar butt sporting the silver Cuban label. Not many people smoked these. Suddenly, his whole body began to tingle. Could this have belonged to the guy who had shot the gambler? All the rat had to do was step through the curtain during the pandemonium that followed and drop Chad's gun nearby. Find out who smoked these cigars and he had his killer.

He peered around. Luckily, Chalky Bell was nowhere to be seen. 'Chalky not around?' he enquired of his replacement, a mousy character who went by the appropriate name of Weasel Wooster.

'He arrived earlier in a right sweat claiming he had to go out,' the man innocently replied. 'Reckoned some urgent business had just come up. When I protested that we were busy, he gave me a right mouthful.'

Troy scowled. Bell was one of the main instigators against a posse being formed. Now he had skedaddled lickety-split. Suspicion showed in the lawman's stiff bearing. It was becoming clear that he was in league with the rustlers. 'You recognize this stub?' he rasped.

Weasel didn't hesitate. 'Only guy who smokes those around here is Stick Drago. He has them specially sent in. Don't like them myself but. . . .'

Troy cut off the idle witter with a shake of his hand. So now he had the name of the killer. 'Ever heard tell of a place called The Kingdom?' he snapped.

The barman saw the grim determination in the marshal's lowered gaze, the fixed set of his tight jawline, and knew this was serious and involved his boss. 'I've heard mention of the place. But nobody I know ever goes up there.'

'How do I reach it?'

'Head due north into the foothills. When you see a rock formation shaped like an Indian head dress, you're in the right area. That's as far as I know. Chalky would know. But he ain't here.' The man shrugged. 'Guess you'll have to trust to luck.'

Troy thanked the barman and disappeared back the way he had come. There was no more information to be found here. But at least he had acquired hard evidence that Buzz Moran had been behind Fairplay's death. Along with April's testimony, that should be enough to clear her brother. He could only hope that he would pick up a trail near Indian Rock that would lead him to the rustler gang's hideout.

Moments later, the marshal was heading north. Alone and trekking into unknown territory he knew that rescuing Chad Prescott and foiling Dooley and his bunch would be a tough proposition. He could only hope that luck and a steely determination would be enough to bring him through unscathed. Any cynicism dogging his thoughts about pinning on the tin star had been cast aside. A solid and unwavering resolve to foil Sheb Dooley's ambitions found him spurring the bay up to a steady canter.

As the crenulated skyline of the Blue Boar foothills

drew ever closer, he fervently prayed for that lucky break he needed to find the illusive Kingdom. Two hours passed. Indian Rock was behind him. Yet thus far, no sign of an entrance to The Kingdom had been forthcoming. Would he ever find it? Or was he destined to lose himself amidst this wild terrain? Troy's previous exhilaration had plummeted as doubts crept in that he had taken on too much.

Cresting a low knoll, his keen gaze spotted a plume of dust up ahead. A lone rider was heading his way. All of a sudden the melancholy of moments before had lifted. Fortunately, the sun was at Troy's back and shining directly into the oncoming rider's eyes. He pulled off the trail into a small cluster of cottonwoods.

Five minutes later, the sound of hoof beats heralded the guy's approach. The steady rhythm indicated he was totally unaware of having been seen. Judging the moment right, Troy pulled out in front of the man forcing him to rein up. The unwavering Colt Frontier ensured that no resistance was forthcoming.

FOURTEEN

UNFINISHED BUSINESS

'Well if it ain't Chalky Bell,' declared the marshal briskly, yet with a distinctively ironic bite. 'And what might you be doing out in this remote quarter? Fella could get himself lost in these hills.'

The barman quickly recovered from the shock of being stopped. 'Nothing wrong with a guy taking a ride, is there? I do this quite often.'

'Nothing at all.' The marshal's upbeat manner then instantly changed to a rasping allegation. 'Except for the fact that Weasel Wooster claimed you lit out in an almighty hurry leaving him alone at a busy time. Mighty strange I'd say. In fact, my bet is that you've just been visiting your cronies up in The Kingdom.' The startled expression told Troy all he needed to know. 'You're in with the rustlers, ain't you buster? And you came out here to warn them of my return from the dead.'

'That's a damned lie,' the barman complained. 'I've just told you. I came out here to exercise my horse. He don't get much, me being a barman.'

Troy wasted no more time arguing. 'Don't give me that nonsense.' He leaned across and whacked the guy over the head with his revolver. Bell tumbled out of the saddle. He was only dazed. But weak enough for Troy to disarm him. 'I know full well you've just come from The Kingdom.'

The lawman's gritted teeth and cold regard told the sly bartender that no amount of smooth talking would get him out of this predicament. All Bell could do was glower at his captor. The jabbing revolver accompanied by a raised fist was adequate persuasion for Bell to submit. 'So what happens now?' he mumbled.

'That's better,' Troy replied dragging his captive up off the ground where he had fallen. 'I knew you'd see sense. You're going to lead me back there.'

'If'n I play ball, will you see that the court goes easy on me?' he pleaded.

'We'll talk about that when I've done what I came out here for.' Troy had no intention of making any promises to this lowlife felon. 'OK let's go. You can give me the word when we're getting close. And just remember. Should you decide to play me false, this revolver is pointed right at your back.'

Half an hour passed before Bell drew to a halt. He pointed to a narrow ravine up ahead. 'That's the southern entrance to The Kingdom. The rebranded cattle are herded out at the far end. The cabin is located in a shallow draw beyond a broken line of rocks. They will have posted a guard up there.'

The crooked bartender was being surprisingly helpful. 'You've done well, Chalky. It'll go in your favour when these skunks have been corralled. Now shuck out the saddle. This is as far as you go. And I'll take your hat and coat.'

Bell gave the order a puzzled frown but did as bidden. Coming out of this dire predicament with a whole skin was all that mattered now.

Early on Troy had noticed the fashionable cut of the barman's coat. It gave him a distinctive appearance. Burgundy velvet with black lapels and gold buttons topped by a grey Stetson with matching red band. An acuity that was going to greatly assist his entry to the outlaw stronghold. Having donned the garish clothes, the marshal hooked out a pair of handcuffs and manacled the morose barkeep to a tree branch. 'This is to make sure you'll still be here when I come back.'

His smile resembled that of a hungry coyote as he nudged the bay over to the ravine. Inside it was so narrow he could reach out and touch both walls. They were cold due to never having felt the warmth of the sun. Sheer rock faces soared up preventing any light from entering the gloomy cutting.

The strange funnel terminated after two hundred yards, opening out into an undulating grass sward dotted with Joshua trees and soaring organ pipe

cacti. The ground climbed steadily towards the line
of broken rocks mentioned by Chalky Bell. Troy
smiled. So far so good. He could now readily appreciate why this hidden valley offered the perfect
hideout for a hard-nosed gang of rustlers. He pushed
onward, keeping a sharp eye open for the expected
sentinel.

He did not have long to wait. Fireball was on
watch. He stepped out from behind a boulder to
greet the unexpected return of Chalky Bell. 'You
leave something in the cabin?' he asked all innocent-
like.

Troy had kept his head down for the wide hat brim
to conceal his face. On reaching the ingenuous
guardian, he dived out the saddle and sent the guy
sprawling. Taken completely unawares, Fireball
stood no chance as Troy leapt to his feet. A solid right
hook followed up by a left to the exposed jaw
knocked the stuffing out of him. 'On your feet,
buster, you're coming with me.' Troy's revolver
ensured the full co-operation of the cowed rustler.
'How far to your hideout in The Kingdom?'
Momentarily, Fireball displayed some resistance.
'Find out for yourself,' he snarled. Troy was in no
mood for stalling tactics. He swiped the barrel of his
gun across the rustler's head with just enough force
to show he meant business. 'I won't ask you again.'

Fireball was squashed. 'Just over that rise, about
fifty yards further,' he muttered dejectedly. The
jabbing gun barrel forced him to move ahead of his
captor. Five minutes later, the cabin swam into view.

Four horses were tied up outside. Troy surmised that Sheb Dooley and his pard were inside. The third horse must belong to Chad Prescott. So who owned the fourth? Troy sat his prisoner down in the cover of some palo verde trees. He needed time to figure out how to get the drop on the killers without harming Chad.

Inside the cabin, Dooley was stamping about in a bad mood. Bell's revelation that Garrison was still very much alive had not gone down well. His anger was aimed at old Ironhand Joplin accusing him of being too darned slow with the rebranding. The virulent complaint in no way intimidated the expert brand forger.

'This latest bunch of steers ain't wearing no simple marks,' the oldster countered with verve. 'Altering a Rocking Chair needs a precise hand to turn it into the Oxbow. You think you can do any better, go ahead and try.'

The two men locked eyes. Dooley was seething at being talked down to by a hired hand. With some effort he managed to stifle any further outburst. He conceded that the old reprobate was right and his expertise was essential. Now was not the time to lose his rag and play the bossman card.

Once Garrison had been dealt with, he would make this old coot pay the price of challenging his authority. Fireball would give him plenty of warning if by some chance the lucky bastard found the entrance to The Kingdom.

But for now the hand of compromise had to be

offered. Accordingly, with some degree of reluctance he relented. 'Sorry for sounding off like that. Do the best you can, Ironhand,' he conceded, yet still intent on maintaining the pecking order. 'But hurry it up. We need to get this last batch in with the regular herd before that damned marshal comes sniffing around.'

Dooley then threw a scornful grimace towards his prisoner. Chad was ashen-faced and sweating like a pig. At first he had refused point blank to co-operate. Dick Blezzard had used a heated running iron to scare the shit out of the arrogant whelp. The sight of the three-fingered outlaw stabbing a haunch of venison with the hissing iron and the promise that he would be next on the menu was enough inducement for him to write out a transfer deed.

'Now that wasn't so hard, was it?' Dooley scoffed, eyes glittering wildly as he once again flourished the scrawled affidavit in the kid's face. He would have a proper one prepared in due course. Chad was breathing hard. His mind was still dwelling on the agony he had only just avoided. Now the young rancher had signed the Oxbow over to him, Dooley knew he was in full control.

Troy stiffened when he saw the fourth man emerge from the cabin. He was an old jasper, grizzled and with a beard to match. He mounted up and rode off towards the north. The fuming lawman ripped the gag off Fireball's mouth. 'Who's the old guy?' he snapped out.

'That's Ironhand Joplin,' the subdued rustler said.

155

'He might appear over the hill, but where changing brands is concerned, there ain't nobody to beat him.' The declaration was uttered with a hint of pride and respect. 'That old jasper has been more like kin to me than my own waster of a father.'

Troy was not impressed. 'He's a no-account rustler, just like you, and will pay the full penalty when I'm done here.' He dragged the guy to his feet and pushed him out into the open, acting as a shield. 'Tell Dooley to come outside, you have some important news.' A rasping growl ensured the rustler complied. 'Any hint of a double-cross and you're crow bait.'

Fireball swallowed nervously. 'You in there, boss?' he called out in a faltering voice. 'I've found out something you need to hear.'

The two desperadoes hustled out of the cabin. For a moment, Dooley failed to spot the lawman hidden behind his prisoner. 'What's so darned urgent you had to leave your post?' he queried. 'It better be good.'

Then he received a shock as Troy Garrison made his presence known. 'I've gotten you bums covered. Now drop your gunbelts and reach!' With an arm encircling Fireball's neck, he edged closer, the revolver in clear view. But neither of the startled rustlers made a move to submit. Shock at this disruption to their plan momentarily confounded the blackguards.

Dooley was the first to recover, volubly cursing the inept sentinel before turning his attention to the

156

trickster. A rancid grin split his sneaky profile. 'You really are becoming a thorn in my butt, Garrison,' he observed lightly. 'But thorns can be pulled. No crummy starpacker is gonna wreck my plans.' He gestured for Blezzard to move over to his left for a better view of their concealed adversary.

It was a stand-off. But Garrison still held the best hand. Though maybe not for long. His advantage was about to be thwarted. At that moment Chad Prescott emerged from the cabin offering Dooley a heaven-sent opportunity to reverse the odds against him. He grabbed the kid. 'Now it's me calling the shots, tin star.' He knew that Troy would in no way place the young rancher's life at risk. 'Toss your hogleg aside.'

The evil grins cloaking the faces of the ruthless outlaws put the fear of Old Nick into the worried Fireball. He could see that his own life was now at risk. 'Don't shoot, boss. You might hit me.'

'A risk you'll have to take,' the heartless villain snarled. 'Get him, Fingers!'

Blezzard's gun erupted striking the rustler hostage in the chest. Before the dead weight could fall to the ground, Troy hung on, swinging the body round as another bullet thudded into the corpse. His own gun now spoke. Blezzard was in the open and stood no chance. He staggered back crashing into his partner, throwing Dooley off balance.

Prescott was not slow in taking advantage of this sudden reversal of fortunes. He knocked the gun out of Dooley's hand and snatched it up ready to finish the outlaw off. Troy stayed his rash action with a sharp directive. 'Don't do it, Chad! This is between me and him now.' Troy dropped the dead Fireball and moved towards a scowling Sheb Dooley. His gun hand was rock steady. 'Stick his hogleg back in the holster then step away.' Chad carefully did as bidden.

'Me and Mr Dooley have some unfinished business that needs tidying up.' His trenchant gaze never faltered as he stopped ten feet from this most abhorrent of foes. 'I'm giving you a fifty-fifty chance to rule your very own kingdom. That's more than you would ever have given me. Reckon you're up to the challenge, mister?'

Dooley's right hand flexed. Since leaving Aguilar he had grown in stature, if only as a lawless brigand. And he knew he was not in the same league when it came to gunfighting prowess. But one derisory tin star was not going to stand in his way. He hunched down ready to make his play. Ridicule soured his warped features as he tried to unsettle the marshal. 'Only a fool plays by those rules.'

And to prove his claim, Dooley clenched his right hand. A tiny Derringer immediately seemed to jump into his palm. It was a trick he had learned from a cheating gambler in Raton. On that occasion the mechanism had jammed and it was the tin horn who ended up in the cemetery. But Dooley had commandeered the sly advantage for just such an occasion as this. At that limited range he couldn't miss. The single .41 calibre bullet erupted from the small barrel.

That would have been the end of the unequal

contest had not the wily lawman been expecting just such a piece of lowdown skulduggery from his devious opponent. All his attention had been focused on Dooley's eyes. If anything would give away the scheming rat's potential for trickery it was inside those black-hearted orbs.

A lifted brow as the body tensed found Troy shifting to one side. The bullet whistled past his left ear. So close it clipped the lobe. Blood spurted from the wound. Knowing his sneaky ploy had failed, Dooley grabbed for his holstered gun. It rose, the hammer snapping back. But no further. With two bullets Troy's Colt Frontier terminated Sheb Dooley's sovereign ambitions in The Kingdom. The .44 hunks of lead slammed into the outlaw's bulky frame.

Nobody moved as a heavy silence descended over the remote enclave. But there was still work to be done. The other rustlers would have heard the gunfire. How would they react? Always the capable lawman, Troy shrugged off the mind-numbing effect of all these killings. 'How many more of these skunks are still to be accounted for?' His brusque query snapped the young rancher out of his own shock-induced state.

'As well as Ironhand Joplin, there are two others,' Chad eagerly replied, relieved that his harrowing experience was finally at an end. 'They're up the far end of the valley finishing off the rebranding. But my guess is that when they heard all the gunfire, they won't hang around. Those guys are just hired hands. They'll disappear into the hills and go seek out some other outfit elsewhere.'

'I'll go check it out just the same. You head back to the ranch. I told April to wait there until I returned.' Troy hesitated before adding somewhat coyly, 'You could tell her that I'd like to stick around . . . that is if'n certain folks don't object to my presence.'

For the first time in a long while, a broad grin spread over Chad Prescott's face. He offered the reluctant tin star a meaningful wink. 'Knowing April, I reckon she'll be the first to invite you over for supper. But there's one thing I need to do before I leave.' He then extracted the transfer deed from Dooley's pocket and applied a lighted match. 'Time for a fresh start, thanks to you, Marshal.'